Sometimes the monsters are real...

For Tor and Skald this is their first viking raid, and their minds are full of thoughts of honor and glory. What awaits them are beasts - huge, hairy and fanged, the Alma will not suffer intruders in their domain. When the Vikings slaughter a female Alma they soon find themselves in the middle of a bloody revenge. Now they must stand and be counted, for their destinies await in the mountains, where the hairy ones dance.

Praise for Berserker

I highly recommend Berserker to anyone looking for a fast, fun and exciting horror story that is as well-written as it is original. - SCOTT WHITMORE

The narrative crashes over you like a tidal wave, punches you like a mailed fist and carries you along with joyful, gory abandon. This book is meant to be consumed with gusto.-INNSMOUTH FREE PRESS

...maintains a delicate balance between character development, plot and brutal action. BERSERKER is an intelligent, fast-paced pulp fantasy novel! William Meikle writes to turns conventions on their heads. - PAGE HORRIFIC

Once again Willie Meikle has crafted a first class adventure story, the narrative rushes along like a Viking Longboat caught in a strong tail wind. That's not to say that Willie skimps on characterisation and plot. The story is peppered throughout with Viking mythology which adds to the reading enjoyment. Not that there was any doubt that this was going to be a great read, I mean Vikings verses Yeti, you know that's going to be a killer book. - GINGER NUTS OF HORROR

Gryphonwood Books by William Meikle

BERSERKER

William Meikle

Gryphonwood

Berserker
Copyright 2010, 2016 by William Meikle
Published by Gryphonwood Press
www.gryphonwoodpress.com

This book is a work of fiction. All characters and situations are products of the author's imagination. Any resemblance to actual persons and events is entirely coincidental.

ISBN-10: 1-940095-44-1
ISBN-13: 978-1-940095-44-8

From the Author

Vikings vs Yeti. What more do you need to know? Actually they're ALMA. Same beasts, different name.

Big beasties fascinate me.

Some of that fascination stems from early film viewing. I remember being taken to the cinema to see The Blob. I couldn't have been more than seven or eight, and it scared the crap out of me. The original incarnation of Kong has been with me since around the same time.

Similarly, I remember the BBC showing re-runs of classic creature features late on Friday nights, and THEM! in particular left a mark on my psyche.

I've also got a Biological Sciences degree, and even while watching said movies, I'm usually trying to figure out how the creature would actually work in nature - what would it eat? How would it procreate? What effect would it have on the environment around it?

On top of that, I have an interest in cryptozoology, of creatures that live just out of sight of humankind, and of the myriad possibilities that nature, and man's dabbling with it, can throw up.

Back at the movies again, another early influence was the Kirk Douglas / Tony Curtis movie THE VIKINGS. There's that, and when I was very young I would be taken ten miles over the hill to the shore at Largs on the Ayrshire coast. There's a memorial there to The Battle of Largs where Scots fought off Vikings. The story was told to me so often it sunk into my soul, and as kids we spent many a day in pretend swordfights as Vikings (when it wasn't Zorro - but that's another story

All those things were going round in my head when I first sat down to write BERSERKER. And there might be some of THE THIRTEENTH WARRIOR in there too.

1

Tor Tyrsson peered against sleet that lashed like a whip against his face, trying to will land into sight. But yet again, for the thirtieth day in succession, all that could be seen was icy water and thick slush. Sailing the *Drakenskin* through it was like trying to make headway through a bath of milk and oatmeal, but going back would mean only more of the same. And going back was not an option. They had only caught one small whale to show for the whole trip so far -- eight barrels of oil from sixty days of Viking. They would be laughed out of Ormsdale if they returned now.

He could only just make out the dim outlines of the other two boats, the *Windmaister* and the *Firewyrm*, slightly behind and to his right. It helped knowing they were there, that somewhere nearby there were two other Viking on watch and currently as miserable as he was.

He pulled his cloak around him and turned his back to the wind. His hands, even inside the deerskin mittens, felt like the ice had already eaten them. His cloak was drenched through from the hood to the bottom that hung, sodden on the wet deck.

And it was some way yet until he'd be relieved.

It is my own fault. I wanted this.

He smiled ruefully to himself, remembering all the nights spent dreaming of Viking, all the times he had pestered his mother for stories about father's travels. If she'd told him the truth of the matter, that it was many days, all the same, of foul weather and wet clothes, he might have stayed in the relative warmth of the halls of Ormsdale.

But this summer past his shoulders had got wide enough that they stopped his passage through the

Riven Rock on the Eastern Shore, and the Thane announced in the Great Hall that Tor was to go on his first Viking. He'd waited two years for this chance. It would be churlish now to wish it away because of a bout of bad weather.

He looked along the length of the boat. Only the Captain moved back there, checking the ropes and the sail. Most of the crew sat huddled along the deck, trying to find warmth in beakers of mutton stew -- all except Tor who kept watch, and one other, who was not welcome among the men.

"Doom," a voice said from the deck below him. "Doom awaits us all."

Tor knew what was coming next.

There was a clatter, bone against bone. He did not have to look down to know that Skald had cast the runes. That too had been a constant for the last thirty days.

"Doom," Skald said.

"Be quiet Skald," Tor said. "Please. No more."

But Orjan Skald was lost in the wyrd with the Norn. There would be no stopping him, not till the wyrd had run its course and he could give the telling.

Not that we have to wait. It will be the same telling as has been told these past thirty days.

"Doom," Skald said again.

"If you say that just one more time," Tor said. "I swear I will give you such a skelp that your head will ring for days to come."

There was a laugh behind him.

"Ignore him boy, Skalds are all the same. Doom, destruction and more doom. That is what they deal in. Better to trust in your axe and your brother Viking."

Tor turned to face the speaker. His Captain, Per Johansson, loomed over Skald. His wolf cloak and fur hood made him look like a great bear ready to attack, and suddenly Tor himself felt the cold chill of the Norn's touch.

The Doom is coming. I too can feel it.

Per laughed again, and shining fragments of ice tinkled in his long beard.

"We all feel a touch of it lad," he said. "It is what comes of being on a boat for so long without women and with no one to fight but ourselves. This is your first voyage. Best get used to it, for there are likely to be many more days like these ahead of you."

"I just wish we could find some land. I need solid ground beneath my feet."

"Ground? What kind of Viking are you?" Per said. His voice, like his laugh, was loud and booming. "Only woman and old men pine for land."

"Land," Skald said at Per's feet.

"Be quiet Skald," Tor said softly, but when he looked down he saw that the wyrd had gone. Orjan Skald's eyes were clear, and he was looking out towards the horizon.

"No," Skald said. "Land. Look."

Just visible through the sleet, a darker shadow in the gloom, high cliffs loomed. Per clapped Skald on the shoulder.

"You promise us *doom* and give us land," he said. "Mayhap I was right to bring you after all."

The Captain left the two youths in the bow and went to rouse the crew.

Tor punched Skald on the shoulder, and Skald smiled ruefully.

"Did I speak of doom again?" Skald asked.

Tor nodded.

"Doom yesterday, doom today, most probably doom tomorrow. That is all the wyrd sends you?"

Skald didn't reply.

Tor thought that Skald looked even paler than

usual, but kept quiet. A Skald's life is not an easy one, and Orjan hadn't asked for it. Only three years ago they had both been no more than boys getting underfoot in the Great Hall in Ormsdale, watching Per and his men wenching and drinking and wondering what both would be like. Tor had since found out, but the incident that made Orjan into the Skald meant that they would never share those pleasures together.

Tor remembered the day well, and dreamed about it often.

Tor's mother threw them from the house that autumn morning and told them to fetch some firewood. It was a request she'd made many times of the boys, and one they always heeded, for it meant they could explore the slopes above Ormsdale without fear of reproach. And they got to take the hand-axe with them.

Tor carried it. He always did, by virtue of being bigger, stronger, and a full week older than his friend. But Orjan was the faster, both in wits and in fleet of foot, and was usually halfway up the scree slope to the tree line while Tor struggled in the lower reaches. Tor often found Orjan watching him from atop a large rock that perched at the top of the hill, resting while Tor struggled upwards getting hotter and more irritated.

The boys had been warned frequently that the slope was unstable, but they were boys and warnings like that matter little when you are young and have many years ahead of you.

That morning the first indication Tor had of a problem was when a small avalanche of gravel and rock ran around his feet. The large rock had toppled off its precarious perch and now bounced down the hill towards him. Tor only just got out of its way in time. It hit an outcrop just beneath him, and shattered into fragments.

"That was lucky," he called out, but got no response. He looked up the hill, only to see Orjan tumbling in a river of stones towards him, head over heels and limp as a dead fish. His friend landed, half buried in scree and gravel at the foot of the hill. Grey stone was splattered with blood.

When Tor reached Orjan he feared the worst. One leg was bent and broken such that bone showed through in his thigh, and his head was crushed on the left side. Tor felt fragments of skull, scalp and blood shift beneath his fingers when he bent to check. He had to bend further to find out whether the boy was still breathing. There was a moment of blind panic when he could find no sign of life, but when he put a hand on Orjan's chest he felt the boy's heart shudder and thump, like a berserker drumming before battle. He stood to run for help, but the people from the edge of town were already running towards them, his mother, face white with shock, in the lead.

That night was the longest of Tor's young life. Gefjun Fjölkunnga, the healer, was sent for, and she spent two long hours tending to Orjan. When she was done, she looked almost as pale as the boy, and declared that the matter now lay with the Nord. She made a brew of hvönn and told them to feed it to him every hour, whether he desired it or not.

Debate raged in the Great Hall whether to send the boy to the Gods early, or let them have him in the morning anyway. There seemed to be little other choice. A fever already burned in Orjan. Gefjun had set his leg, but all that saw him knew that the boy would never run again, and might not even walk. That was a small matter though, for it seemed almost sure that his mind was gone, to wander dark places before his body could catch up. Three women took turns all that night tending him. Tor slept at the foot of the bed and would not be moved, even under threat of a whipping.

The Gods were kind. They sent Orjan back; bent and broken, and no longer *just* Orjan, but they sent him back.

His healing was long and hard, but Tor saw to it that the other youths could not torture this *weakness* in their midst. Orjan Skald stuck to Tor's side wherever he went. And if he knew that he was spoken of throughout Ormsdale as *Tor's pet,* he never mentioned it.

When Per Johansson called for Viking to go east, Tor was among the first to volunteer, and there was never any doubt that the Skald would go as well. And if some of the crew were not in favour, Per himself took the youth under his personal protection, and Per's right hand was strong enough to keep the peace. For a while at least.

If only he would stop pronouncing doom at every turn.

Skald struggled to his feet. Tor put out a hand, offering help but Skald knocked it away and used his staff to clamber upright. Tor saw how much pain just that act had cost, but said nothing.

They stood there, side by side, and watched the land grow closer.

"Land at last," Tor said. "I wonder what waits us there?"

"I'm not sure I want to know," Skald said softly.

They sailed alongside a high cliff for several hours, a wall of grey stone with no vegetation, no gulls. Waves hit the walls and boomed, like distant thunder, throwing spray in the wind that lashed into their faces alongside the sleet. The boat yawed and pitched as the waves rebounded off the cliffs and threw the water into high hills and deep valleys. The tops of the cliffs were lost from sight under low cloud, and everything looked a flat dead grey.

"Not much to trade with here, eh lad?" Per said at Tor's shoulder.

He had the dogs with him. Two tall rangy wolfhounds, Huginn and Muninn, excited to have been let out of the hold, got up on their rear legs to look over the bow, their tails wagging excitedly.

"They can smell the land," Per said as the dogs howled in unison. "And like yourself, are eager to feel ground under their feet."

"And a tree to pish on?"

Per laughed.

"Aye. That too," the big man said, and clapped Tor on the shoulder again. "When we reach a spot to land, you shall be first ashore. It is your right, on your first Viking."

"No, he will not. I will not allow it"

Tor recognised the voice before he turned towards it. Kai Persson stood there with three others. Tor barely knew their names. The fact that they followed Kai as closely as the wolfhounds followed Per told him all he needed to know about them.

Lapdogs hoping to pick up scraps from their master.

Kai carefully brushed his plaited hair away from his face. Despite the driving sleet he did not wear a cloak.

Of course not. It would obscure that shiny new breastplate he is so proud of.

"It is *my* right to be first ashore Father," Kai said. "You will not deny me it."

Per didn't even look round. He threw out his right hand and smacked Kai in the mouth. The heavy leather glove split his top lip. It burst like a too-soft fruit and blood flew in the sleet. One of the three *lapdogs* reached for a sword, but when Per turned the look on his face was enough to quieten them.

"Your right?" he said, shouting in Kai's face. "You had the right last year. And what did you do with it? You fell on your hind-end in the surf."

Kai looked like he might speak again, but Per raised his hand, and once more there was quiet.

Skald laughed.

"*Down boy*," he said.

Kai stepped forward and aimed a kick at Skald, but it didn't connect, for before it landed both wolfhounds had leaped forward and clamped their teeth on the Viking's ankle. Per let them chew for a second before ordering them off.

"Huginn, Muninn. Heel."

"Aye," Skald said, laughing again. "Put him down. You do not know where he has been."

Tor put a hand on Skald's shoulder to quieten him.

"Excuse him," Tor said to Kai. "His mouth moves faster than the wind, and with as little thought to consequence."

Kai spat a glob of blood at Skald's feet.

"There are far too many of your *pets* on board this boat," he said to Per. "It would be best to take good care of them. You would not want one to go missing in the night."

He limped off, his three henchmen keeping close order behind him.

"Kai is correct," Tor said. "He is your son. It is his right to be first ashore."

Per watched the four Viking huddle in conversation under the sail.

"Kai cannot find his arse when he needs a shite," he said. "The honour will be yours. I will hear no more on it."

Per strode off. The dogs barked once, as if saying goodbye to the land, and as ever left to follow at their master's heels. Once Per passed the four others under the sail, Kai turned to Tor, and made a motion of moving a knife across his throat.

Skald laughed again.

"Same old Kai. Still hungry for attention. Still stupid."

Tor shook his head.

"Stupid he may be. But he is Per's son. One day he will be Captain. It will be best to be on good terms with him."

"He has no time for your *good terms*. He never has. You know that."

Yes. I know that. From long and painful experience.

Two hours sailing later they came to the mouth of a high wide fjord.

"Well Tor," Per said, coming once more to join him at the prow. "What do you think? Are there rich pickings to be had? Or is calmer water a good enough reason to sail awhile between these hills?"

"It would be good to get out of this sleet?" Tor said hopefully, bringing a laugh from the Captain.

"That it will lad, that it will."

Per ordered the boats inside. Here in the lee of the eastern cliff they finally found some shelter from the wind and the sleet, and they were able to make good time. And in the sheltered inlet, they also found forests lining the hillsides.

"Well, the dogs at least shall be happy with so many trees available," Per laughed.

High above a pair of white-tailed eagles soared in a slow dance.

Per clapped his hands.

"Where eagles fly, there is always food to be had nearby," he said. "Fish, fowl and maybe even coney."

"Something other than old hard mutton in any

case," Tor muttered.

The fjord was longer than any Tor had previously encountered, and seemed to stretch for many miles into the far misty distance. But finally, two whole months after they had left Ormsdale, they found signs of people.

It wasn't much at first, just some fishing nets strung across inlets on the shore, and a solitary ruined building that looked like it had once stood guard halfway down the fjord.

"It's a ruin," Skald said. "Whoever built it has long gone."

Per smiled.

"It may only be a ruin to you lad, but to me it is an omen. For if they have had to build reinforced dwellings, they must have something to protect," he said. "Mark my words, there will be a settlement at the end of this fjord. And there we shall see what we shall see."

Per was proved right twenty minutes later when they passed a jutting headland and had their first clear view down the remaining length of the fjord. Snow covered mountains dominated the far end, a tall range of them heading off into the misty distance. Beneath the nearest peak, almost hidden in shadow, sat a settlement of small roundhouses. Smoke rose from several of the roofs.

"Make ready," Per shouted, and the air filled with noise; the din of metal on metal and the clash of spears as the Viking prepared.

"I thought we were on a trading mission?" Skald said.

Per laughed.

"When they see us coming, most assume the worst. Tis best to be ready for a less than warm reception."

Skald left for a short time. On his return he brought

Tor his tall two-handed battleaxe and his helm. Tor had to brush ice and sleet from his hair to get the helm to fall into place, and the axe handle felt slick and cold in his palm when he removed the mittens.

"You should have a sword," Skald said.

"Only when I earn one," Tor replied. "And when Odin wills it."

He hefted the axe.

"Besides," he said. "This was good enough for my father. It will do for me."

They came up on the settlement fast. Ahead of them was a small rocky shore with two old fishing boats pulled up above the tide line.

Tor realised he had started to breathe heavily, and fought to calm himself.

I have wanted this moment for years. I will not hurry so quickly that I miss the enjoyment of it.

He looked ahead of the boat, planning the spot where he might best enter the water. As he surveyed the shoreline there was no sign of any people.

"Where are they?" Skald whispered. "Someone *must* have seen us."

"Maybe they fear us?" Tor said. "Mayhap they are in hiding."

"And fear us they should," Per shouted at his side, unsheathing his long sword.

He raised it in the air.

"We are Viking," he roared.

"We are Viking," the crew shouted as one, and Tor leaped over the side into the water.

2

Skald watched Tor leap off the longboat with a mixture of pride and envy.

I should be beside him.

He pushed the thought away. Pity was for the weak. And Skald was far from weak, no matter what the others may think of him. Yes, his body had been broken and his left leg was of use only as something to stand on. Yet he had overcome that enough to be allowed on this voyage, enough to think of himself as *Viking*, in mind if not in body.

He kneaded the thin muscle at his thigh, trying to get heat into it, but it was like a cold stone against the bone, with about as much flexibility.

I will never sit in Valhalla. The spoils of battle will not be mine.

He had known that ever since the day he woke to a world where everything was pain. Since then there had been a great many days when he felt like taking himself to a cliff-top and giving his body to the sea. Strangely, it was the wyrding that gave him the will to carry on, even as it drained all strength from him.

He had only been out of bed two days when the wyrd hit him for the first time. They thought it was a fit, a sign that his mind was too ill to heal. But Orjan knew otherwise, for he had seen dark things while away with the Norn, things that had not yet come to pass.

Tor's father Tyr stood on the deck of a longboat as they fought a storm that had lashed up giant waves; waves that loomed like hills above even the height of the mast. Sea spume flew like white spittle all around his head, but he kept his gaze straight ahead, for one momentary loss of concentration would mean death for them all in this storm.

The wooden deck creaked and complained as they tried to get the dragon's head of the prow to point into the wind, to at least get her onto an even keel. But it was not to be. The seventh wave hit them side on and the longboat rolled, banking so far sideways that the starboard edge of the keel was almost completely in the sea. They had only just started to roll back when the largest wave so far crashed down on them from above and filled the boat with water.

The mast snapped. A long spar fell like a great spear thrown by Thor himself and cleft through Tyr from neck to groin. He did not even have time to die before the next wave washed him overboard and the sea took him straight to Valhalla.

Skald had woken from that one clutching at his chest and screaming, but it was Tor who came to him first, and he could not speak of what he had seen, not to his friend. So he had held his counsel, even as Tyr took the longboat on Viking two weeks later.

And two weeks after that, the news came, as he knew it would.

He never told Tor what he had seen, but the guilt ate away at him, destroying part of what their friendship had once been, a part that he would never get back, a part that had been as important to him as the use of his left leg.

I survived. The Norn spared me. They spared me for a reason.

That much had become plain on the night the wyrd called him for the second time. On this occasion he did not have the luxury of being able to keep silent, for it called him right at the end of his recitation. He was standing at the head of the Thane's table in the Great Hall, reciting the tale of Ragnar Hairy-Breeks. He managed to get through the section on the Viking

King's raid on the Frankish capital, and indeed was almost finished, reciting the famous death speech.

The Æsir will welcome me.
Death comes without lamenting...
Eager am I to depart.
The Dísir summon me home.
Gladly shall I drink ale in the high-seat with the Æsir.
The days of my life are ended.
I laugh as I die.

At which the wyrd took him and Skald fell to the ground. The Viking in the Great Hall laughed and cheered, thinking it a great jest and an apt end to the tale. But Skald never heard, for he was far away, flying in the wyrd.

Even as the cheering died and the hall fell quiet he had stood, eyes rolled up in their sockets, and pointed at the throne where the Thane sat.

He was told later what he had said.

Death-doomed you will soon drink with Ygg
Not long the life left thee.
The Norn wish thee ill.

When he woke, he was face to face with Gefjun Fjölkunnga, the healer. She stared deep into his eyes, then handed him the pouch of bones he carried even now.

"Runecaster," she called him.

But from that day on, he only had one name in Ormsdale.

Skald.

The Thane died two weeks later from an infection of the blood. And since then, the wyrd had been the defining thing of each day, of each hour of his life, no matter how much he might wish otherwise.

The memory of that morning's wyrding came back to him.

It had been stronger than ever before. And it

started, as always, with drums.

They beat, slowly at first, then in an ever-increasing frenzy until his skull threatened to split apart. Behind the drums, wind howled, a raging shriek that grew higher and higher.

Everything was white, a dancing sheet of snow that swirled around him as if alive.

And in the snow, blood. Drops of it at first, like beads of red ice.

Then came a roar, the like of which Skald had never heard.

White turned red as the drums beat a word into his skull.

Doom.

It was with a heavy heart that Skald dropped over the side of the boat. Leaning heavily on his staff he began to make his slow way to the shore.

3

The water reached almost to the top of Tor's thighs and gripped at his balls like a frozen hand, spurring him on faster as he waded towards the shore. Behind him he heard the cries of the crews as they leapt into the sea.

This is what it feels to be a Viking.

All around him men screamed and shouted, and he heard frantic splashing as the others tried to gain on him, tried to be first ashore.

But this was *his* right, and no one would deny him. He put all his effort into forcing his way through the water. He almost fell on coming to a sudden deeper dip, but the thought of Per's ridicule, and the long handle of the axe, kept him upright, and once more he forged ahead.

He was first out of the water, and gave out a shout of triumph that echoed in the mountains above. The only sounds as he walked out of the sea were the splashing of his fellow Viking behind him and the sucking rattle of pebbles around his feet.

He raised his axe, but there was still no sign of any defenders. Huginn and Muninn bounded ashore next to him, soaking him further as they sloughed the water from their hair and tails before running on into the settlement. He whistled to call them back, but he was not Per and they ignored him.

They stopped, sniffed at the nearest building, then cocked their legs and left a stream of hot piss on the stone before moving on. They were soon lost in the jumble of buildings.

Tor stayed in the lead of the Viking as they walked off the beach to the edge of the settlement. As they entered the small town the soft drizzle and sleet turned to snow and wind gusted and whistled around the ridges of his helm.

The houses were all small and squat, little more than circles of rough-hewn stone with crude wooden and straw roofs on top. Fish and kelp lay in long rows on wooden drying platforms all along the shore, and the smell caught at the back of Tor's throat, threatening to make him gag.

"Yes," he heard Kai say behind him. "This certainly looks like the place for rich trade."

"Quiet boy," Per growled. "Or would you like your other lip thickened?"

Tor tried to ignore them. He had been listening for several seconds now, but had heard nothing from the settlement.

He walked over to the closest house. He had to bend to enter through the doorway. The house, no more than a single room with an alcove of straw for a bed, was empty except for what looked like old leather draped on the walls and lain on the floor. There was no sign that the people that lived here had the use of metal. Clay pots and beakers were stacked on stone shelves. One of the pots held sharpened bones of various thickness, from as wide as his thumb down to a fishbone as thin as a hair. A large clay pot steamed over smoking coals, but he couldn't smell what might be in it, as the whole room stank of stale body odour, fish guts and something sour that might be milk long since gone off.

Tor moved to the fire, bent over the pot and sniffed.

Per spoke from behind him.

"Anything lad?"

"Fish stew," Tor said. "A lot of fish stew. But no sign of who made it."

Per nodded.

"They must have seen us coming. They will be hidden somewhere that they think is safe. I have seen this before."

As Tor turned he could see through the door that the snow was coming harder now.

Per joined him in looking out at.

"Yes. We have taken too long on our journey," the Captain said. "We may have to harbour here for the winter. We had best find those that live here. We may have need of whatever food they can share."

Suddenly the room went dark as a figure blocked the doorway.

Kai walked into the hovel.

"Share? Viking do not share. Viking take."

Per turned and stared.

"Viking do what their Captain tells them," Per said, putting his hand on his sword. "Or would you like to dispute that?"

Kai smiled. His lip split and blood started to flow down his chin before he wiped it away.

"Yes. I would."

His three companions stepped through the doorway and stood beside him. Kai put his hand on his sword.

"What say you father? Would you care to have another test of my resolve?"

Per pointed at the split lip.

"Resolve? Is that what you call it?" he said, laughing. "I drew blood last time and you *resolved* to swallow it like a woman."

Kai's hand griped tighter on the hilt of his sword.

"Do not be a fool. Now is not the time to challenge me boy," Per said. "We do not yet know if we are safe here."

Kai didn't speak, merely drew his sword. The other

three did the same.

Tor hefted his axe and stepped up beside Per. Kai saw him and laughed.

"Stand down pup. This is work for men."

Tor looked Kai in the eye.

"Then it is time I showed you who is the man here," he said. "Come, if you have the balls for it."

Kai stood there, sword raised, staring at Tor.

Tor saw indecision in the man's eyes.

And to think I spent my childhood in fear of him.

The three *lapdogs* waited to see what Kai's decision might be.

Tor smiled, and Kai saw it. He stepped forward.

Huginn and Muninn chose that moment to start loud, frantic, barking.

Ignoring Kai's sword completely, Per pushed him aside and headed towards the sound.

"Come on lad," he shouted to Tor. "They have run something to ground. Let us see what their hunt has turned up."

The noise was coming from the eastern side of the settlement, where it came up against the wooded foothills of the mountains beyond. By the time Tor and Per got there, a crowd of Viking had formed around the baying dogs. Whatever the dogs had found, they had it cornered in a cramped area between two houses that looked and smelled like it served as a midden. Tor followed behind Per as the Captain pushed his way through to see what they had.

At first Tor thought it was one of the snow-white bears that sometimes found their way south in harsh winters. But no bear ever looked like this.

The eyes were the first things that Tor noticed. Milky white they were, like icy stones set far back in a skull covered in matted fur that might once have been white but was covered in muck from where the beast had obviously had its head stuck in the midden. The body was covered in more fur, and there the beast was as white as any northern bear.

But it stood upright on two stout legs, and was taller than the tallest Viking, and nearly three feet wide across its broad shoulders. The dogs danced around it, keeping their distance. The beast seemed confused by the barking, and clapped hands as huge as hams across its ears. Its head was oval shaped, the skull slightly tapered at the rear. The hair was thicker there, almost mane-like where it ran down the broad back.

It opened a mouth full of long yellow teeth and screamed.

"Listen to the bitch squeal," one of the Viking shouted.

It was only then that Tor noticed it was female. Huge pendulous breasts hung over a distended belly that hung almost to the beast's knees. Pink nipples the size of Tor's thumb peeked from the fur covered chest.

"Look at the paps on her," someone else shouted. "Do you think she will let us have a feel?"

"You should know," another called out. "She is *your* mother."

When they laughed at that the beast squealed again, and this time there was a piteous note in it that reminded Tor of the night they brought mother the news about father. Suddenly he felt almost sorry for her.

She started to paw, as if trying to catch the sounds the dogs were making. Each massive hand had five fingers tipped with thick broken nails several inches long that raked at the air. The dogs became more and more frantic, barking furiously and darting around just outside the beast's arm's length.

"Huginn, Muninn. Heel." Per shouted. "Come to

heel."

The dogs slunk on their haunches and retreated back towards Tor and Per, but they never took their eyes off the beast. As soon as the hounds stopped barking she calmed. She stood quietly; staring at the semicircle of Vikings that had her hemmed in.

"Now she *is* dangerous," Per said softly.

"What do we do? Let it go?" a man said.

"Yes," Per replied. "Let her go. We have no fight with her kind. She is just a dumb beast looking for food."

"No," Kai shouted. "I did not come all this way to see us let a *troll* go free."

Before Per could stop him Kai stepped forward, swinging his sword. The beast threw up an arm in front of herself, and the sword bit deep into flesh, bringing a gout of hot blood that sprayed the faces of those standing closest.

The beast lowered the arm, and stared at the wound. Tor saw puzzlement in her eyes.

She has never seen an edged weapon before.

Kai stepped forward again, but she had only needed one blow to learn her lesson. Her right arm came round, stiff and straight like a log, catching Kai in the chest and sending him flying into the three men behind him, knocking all four into a heap.

She raised her face to the sky and roared. It was no piteous wailing this time, but a hot blast of fury that made Tor's legs go weak and threatened to send him running.

The Captain looked round at him and winked.

"Stand with me lad," Per said. "We shall have need of that axe."

He turned back and stared at the beast.

She fell still again, staring back at Per, and at the sword in his hand. The big man showed her the weapon, swishing it through the air between them. She looked at her arm, to where blood flowed, matting the fur a deep crimson, then looked back at the sword.

She let out another roar, and moved to one side out of range of the blade. She leaped at the Viking, trying to breach the line.

Two men moved to intercept her, swords raised. She took one look at the weapons, and turned in the other direction.

Three Viking waited there with long spears held in front of them. She broke the spears like so much kindling. The Viking broke in disarray.

She caught one by the arm and set about gutting him with something that Tor thought looked like glee. Her huge hand gouged a massive hole in the man's belly and pulled upwards. He splayed open and his guts fell out in a slithering heap to steam on the snow. A spray of hot blood filled the air, and good men screamed like frightened children. She threw the body aside and jumped, covering ten feet in one leap, landing on Tyg Pytersson's back. The man wailed pitifully as he saw his own arm pulled completely from its socket, and could only look in horror as it was used to pound down into his skull, spraying brain and bone on the fresh snow.

Styg Stygsson didn't even live that long. The beast got hold of his left leg and his right arm, and pulled. What looked like no effort at all left only a pile of bone and flesh on the ground that the beast proceeded to trample into mush, jumping up and down on the spot until all that was left was a red steaming pile of slush.

"Enough," Per shouted, the bellow echoing around them.

He stepped forward and, ducking under a huge swinging arm that would have flattened him if it had hit, he swung his sword, cutting deep into the fur at the beast's shoulder. She turned towards the source of the new pain, and that gave Tor an opening. He stepped up and swung his axe, biting a deep wound at the back of her left leg and bringing her partially to her knees. As she turned and showed him her teeth Per sliced across her back with the broadsword. The blow sent her face-first to the ground.

Tor screamed in triumph, and stepped in again, swinging in a blow that would cleave her skull.

But he had underestimated her. She turned and in one movement grabbed at the axe as it came down. It sheared off two fingers of her left hand, the blood spurting in gouts all over Tor's upper body. But he was too busy to notice, for the beast had wrested the axe from his grasp. He heard the weapon clang on stone as she flung it away, but by that time she was roaring her fury in his face as she threw him to the ground and bent over him.

He felt hot damp breath on his cheeks, and smelled rotting fish. His sight was full of a wet red mouth and thick yellow teeth that looked like old finger bones. He tried to roll to one side, but her weight sat on his chest, and was slowly pushing all life out of him.

Things started to go grey.

Valhalla, I am coming.

But not yet. The weight lifted suddenly and the beast rolled off him. Something brown flashed past him and threw itself at the beast's neck.

Huginn, he thought as he got to his knees, but when he rose he could see that the hounds were by Per's side.

So what has saved me?

The Viking had reformed their semicircle, but they were not attacking. Tor saw why when he turned.

The beast was on her knees on the ground, and someone had wrapped themselves across her back, legs locked under the beast's huge arms. She tried to claw him off, but she was weakening fast, and the man was too far out of reach behind her broad shoulders. A red knife came up, went down, again, and again, and blood flew in the snow. The beast fell forward onto its hands. She raised her head and looked straight at Tor as the life went out of her eyes. The bloody pale face of the brown figure raised his head in a scream as the beast slumped all the way to the ground and finally lay still.

It was only then that Tor recognised Skald.

But this Skald was one that Tor had *never* seen before. The wyrd was on him, that much was obvious, but instead of turning him quiet and withdrawn, this had taken a different turn.

Skald was lost in a blood fury. Gore coated him, from head to thigh, his face streaked red with blood. Although the beast beneath him was long dead, still he brought the knife up and down, pounding it again and again into the red soaked fur.

"Skald!" Tor shouted. "Stop."

The knife paused at the top of the arc.

"Orjan," Tor said softly. "Please?"

The knife fell from Skald's hand. His eyes, shockingly white in the bloodied face, looked straight at Tor without seeing him.

"What has become of you?" Tor said softly.

The other Viking present knew exactly what they were looking at, and the word came on several of their lips.

Berserker.

4

Skald came up out of another dream of blood and doom.

This time the blood stayed with him as the dream faded. It covered his hands, and when he felt his face he found it had coated his cheeks. He tasted it on his lips, and felt it slide and smear under his fingers.

A shadow fell over him and he looked up. Tor stood there, holding out Skald's staff. He took it and used it to pull himself to his feet. He realised he was thick with cooling blood, from head to mid-thigh.

"Am I hurt? Did I have another accident?"

Tor shook his head.

"You saved my life," he said. "Come. Let us get you cleaned up."

Skald turned and looked at the bloody thing on the ground.

"Who died?"

"Never mind," Tor said. "I will tell you later."

The Viking parted to let them through and Skald let Tor lead him away. None of them would look him in the eye, but Skald barely noticed. He felt as he always did when he came out of the wyrd -- weak and disoriented, barely knowing what went on around him.

But I have never brought the blood back with me afore now. What new tricks have the Norn in store for me this time?

Tor led him to one of the huts and sat him on a pile of furs. Skald sat quietly while his friend did his best to clean up the blood and gore that covered him.

"What do you remember?" Tor asked quietly.

"I have been thinking long and hard on that. I remember getting off the boat, and walking in the water. I was so slow that the rest of you were all into the town before I even reached the beach. I heard the dogs barking and headed for the sound and..."

"And?"

Skald shook his head.

Just the same as always.

White and red, drums and doom.

He looked up at Tor.

"You said something about someone saving your life?"

Tor's face broke into its first smile for a while.

"Yes. You did."

Skald dropped his head and looked at his hands. They were still tinged pink, despite all Tor's efforts to clean them.

"Did the wyrd hurt someone? Did *I* hurt someone?"

Tor shook his head.

"Come and see. I cannot get you any cleaner anyway."

Skald had to lean on the stick before he could move. His leg felt like it was made from frozen stone, and he had to drag it behind him. It ached with every step, pounding in time with his heart.

The drum of doom.

The snow fell heavier now, large heavy flakes blowing on a stiff breeze, lying just enough on the muddy ground that their footprints left an impression as they left the hut.

The Viking huddled around something that lay on the ground in a pool of blood. The men were all quiet, subdued, and became even more so when they saw Skald.

Per turned as Tor and Skald approached and motioned them forward.

"Come lads. See what you have done."

Skald stopped and shook his head.

It was not I. Whatever was done, I had no part in it.

Tor pushed at his back.

"Come Skald," he said. "It is dead."

"Aye," Per laughed. "You made *very* sure of that fact."

When Skald first looked down at the body all he could see was blood and gore. But slowly he began to make out features -- the long broken nails, the white fur and the yellow teeth. He wondered if perhaps he was still in some strange corner of wyrd where things were *almost* normal.

"*I* killed that thing?"

"That you did," Tor said. "And you saved my life in doing so. I owe you a debt I may never be able to repay."

Skald could not drag his eyes from the beast.

"What is it?" he whispered.

It was Kai who answered.

"It was a fucking *troll*," he said, and spat on the body. "A fucking *troll bitch*."

Skald noticed that the man's new breastplate wasn't quite so shiny. It had a row of deep gouges from left nipple to right hip and a large dent all across the chest. There was blood at Kai's mouth, though whether from the earlier split lip, or from anything broken inside him it was hard to tell.

We can always hope it is the latter.

Skald looked down at the body again as three men turned it over. It *squelched* as blood and mud sucked at the fur. Pale milky eyes stared accusingly at Skald.

"It does not *look* like a troll," he said.

Kai spat blood again.

"And how many trolls have you seen?"

Skald looked along the length of the body.

"Well, I have never seen one that moves after it has been killed, that is for sure."

The distended belly swelled, moving from within.

Kai drew his sword.

"Never trust a Skald to do the work of a man," he said. He thrust his blade into the beast's belly and started to cut. The squirming became frantic.

Kai's next cut opened the stomach wide, cutting through the muscle. The belly gaped and split. There, in the depths of the gore, three foetuses squirmed, sharp nails trying to rip through flesh, pale teeth chewing at their mother's body as they struggled for birth.

"What fresh shite is this?" Kai said. He bent and lifted a bloody mass from inside the shell of the belly. It was the size of a large cat, and twice as noisy. It squirmed in his hand and squealed.

From somewhere high above them, an answering roar echoed in the cliffs.

Kai looked up. The bloody thing is his hand took its chance and sunk tiny teeth into his wrist. Disgusted, Kai swung around and pounded it against the nearest wall.

It slid, quiet now, to the ground. Beneath Kai the other two newborn pushed themselves free from the gore.

"Bastard things," Kai said, and stood on them. They squirmed underfoot, and one managed to sink sharp teeth into the toe of his boot before he shook it off and stomped them into pulp, over and over, long after they too were still.

"Who is *Berserker* now?" Tor said quietly.

If Kai replied it was lost in the echoing roar of fury that came down from the heights above them.

5

Tor looked up to the high lands above the town. The echoing roar faded and was lost in the wind. It wasn't repeated.

"Bear?"

"It must be," Kai said and kicked at the beast's corpse. "Surely there cannot be two such things in Midgard. Not at the same time."

Per shook his head.

"That was no bear," he said. He pointed at the remains of the dead Viking. "Get these back to the boats. We will see to them later. And let us see if there is anything of worth in this place. I wish to leave as soon as we can. I fear we have overstayed our welcome."

Per looked over to where Kai and his followers stood over the body of the beast. Kai used the point of his sword to prise three-inch teeth from the red maw, collecting trophies.

"You would think he was the one that killed it," Tor said. "The spoils should go to Skald."

"Do you think your friend would want them?" Per said quietly.

Tor shook his head.

"Just wait," Per replied. "When we get back to Ormsdale Kai will have a story ready for the Great Hall about his *heroic* battle against the troll. And he will have the buckled breastplate and the trophies to prove it. But we, we who fought the beast, we will always know the truth of it."

Kai threw a look at Per, but said nothing. Per smiled back at him, then turned to Tor once more.

"Have a look round this place lad," he said. "And take Skald with you. It would be best if he was out of sight for a while."

"What about Kai? He may want to finish what was started earlier."

Per laughed.

"I can handle Kai. Just try to find if there is anyone here."

Per looked at the sky again. It had gone almost white, and snow fell steadily enough to be accumulating thickly on the ground at their feet.

"And do not take long about it," he continued. "I want to be back on the boats within the hour."

Tor had to drag Skald away from the corpse of the beast.

"Truly, I did that?" Skald said, and Tor managed a small laugh.

"Truly," Tor said. "The days when Kai and his dogs play jokes on you are over. They will not dare try anything again. Not after today."

Skald still looked unsure.

"Come away," Tor said. "Per has a task for you."

"For me?"

Tor clapped his friend on the shoulder.

"For us. Come. Let us see what other pleasures this hamlet holds for two men on their first Viking."

Tor and Skald wound through more of the small roundhouses, looking into each.

All were the same – empty, but only recently. Several had fires still smoking, and a few had more fish stew brewing on cauldrons. Each house smelled worse than the last, and each had a midden to the side that smelled worse again; piles of broken shells, fish pieces and frozen shite that looked suspiciously human.

"It seems we have discovered civilisation," Tor said, trying to raise Skald's spirits. His friend's limp was more pronounced than ever, but Tor kept quiet on that subject. He'd learned long ago never to draw attention to the Skald's weaknesses.

Skald had barely spoken since they'd left the other Viking. His face was drained of blood, his lips cold and grey. If he hadn't been upright and walking Tor might have taken him for dead.

Tor wasn't sure he minded the quiet. He could not get the image out of his head, of the wide-eyed fury of the *Berserker* as he pounded the bloody knife into the beast's corpse. He could not equate that *thing* with the friend by his side.

And I do not ever want to.

So they proceeded through the settlement in silence.

They met no one. It was only when they reached the western edge that they found signs of where the people had gone. A muddy trail led away, up towards a rocky outcrop above the bay.

Tor started forward, only for Skald to pull him back.

"No," Skald said. Just that word.

"Why not?"

Skald did not speak, but he looked more frightened than at any time Tor had seen him.

"Doom," Skald whispered.

Tor stopped.

"You have *seen* it? Here? For me?"

Again Skald went quiet. He was looking up, scanning the high cliffs above.

"No," he said finally. "I have heard it. These past thirty days the roaring has been in the wyrd. But now it has come back from there with me, like the blood. I have brought it upon us."

"You have done nothing," Tor said. "Nothing but kill yon beast and save me from an early visit to Valhalla."

Skald shook his head.

"Something has been coming these past thirty days. Coming through me."

Once more Tor knew when to talk, and when to remain silent.

There has never been any reasoning with him when he is like this.

Skald started to shiver. Tor put out a hand to comfort his friend, but once more he was brushed away.

"My heart would ask you not to go any further. But you will go anyway," Skald said. "Because you are Viking."

Tor stood, torn between friend and duty. He looked at Skald, then looked up the hill, following the path of the trail to a large overhanging rock that looked like a skull smiling its death-grin out from the mountain.

I am Viking first, and friend second. I must follow my Captain's order.

"Stay here," he said to Skald. "I will go and check. Just to the large rock. Then I will return. I promise."

"Yes," Skald said, and there was a touch of bitterness in his voice that Tor had never heard before. "Go be Viking. Go running to doom."

Tor headed up the muddy path. He looked back once to see Skald still scanning the high ground, snow falling unnoticed into his face and hair.

The ground got steep quickly, and Tor soon found he had to lean on his axe to push himself upwards. Mud turned to rock underfoot, slippery with freezing slush. Halfway up he stopped to catch his breath and looked down at the settlement.

From here the pattern of the houses could be clearly seen through the blowing snow. They had been built with twelve of them in a rough outer oval, egg shaped with the more pointed end just beneath where

Tor stood. Inside that were six more houses placed in a pattern he almost recognised. It was only when he looked to Skald, still standing silent, then looked back at the settlement, that he realised what it was.

One for each eye, one for the nose, and three for the gaping maw of a mouth. It is the face of the beast.

The whole settlement was indeed laid out in a crude representation of a huge face, one that could only be seen from a height.

Why would they do such a thing?

But speculation would have to wait. The snow was still falling hard, and he did not fancy a return journey downhill if the weather was to worsen. He leaned on the axe and pushed on upwards.

The skull-shaped rock now loomed large above him.

"I am almost there," he called out, and turned a corner. Only to come face to face with a twin rank of pointed stakes that completely blocked the path. The dark mouth of a large cave lay behind the stakes. Three dark-skinned faces peered suspiciously out at him.

"Greetings?" he said.

They stared back at him. They were small people, black haired, with eyes slanted under heavy folds. When he looked closer he saw that their skin wasn't dark at all – it was just that every available area of their faces was covered with tiny tattoos.

"We come in friendship, looking for trade," he said. He showed them the axe. "Trade?"

"Yes," Skald said behind him. "That will work. Can you not see that they are terrified?"

"I did not think you would get up the hill," Tor said.

Skald smiled grimly.

"Getting up hills was always easy. It was the way down that was the problem."

He pushed past Tor, moving the tall axe aside.

"Put that down," Skald said. "We come in friendship, remember?"

Tor stood back and watched with admiration as Skald *talked* to the people in the cave. It was all done with hand actions and mummery, but by the time he screwed up his face, threw out his hands and *roared*, Tor knew that behind the stakes, they knew his meaning exactly.

"*Alma*," one of them replied, and mimicked the roar.

Skald nodded, and Tor understood.

Alma. The beast was an Alma.

The conversation, if it could be called that, continued. Tor soon grew bored, and went to look back down into the settlement. He was dismayed to see that the snow was now so heavy that his view was obscured completely. He could see ten yards of the downward slope, but even that was in danger of being covered in drifting snow.

"Skald," he shouted. "It is time we got on our way."

6

Skald heard Tor's shout, but chose to ignore it. He had the attention of the people in the cave, and didn't want to lose it now.

He'd already learned that the beast was an *Alma*, and the small people hid in the cave to protect themselves from it. He was now trying to persuade them that it was safe, that the *Alma* was dead. They looked incredulous, and refused to believe him, even after he showed them the blood on his cloak and tunic.

He had no idea how many of them were back there, but from the smell, it seemed they were packed in tight. And they had children with them. Two small faces had already peered out at him, and ducked quickly away when he smiled.

They will be back.

Skald was trying to convey the concept of their longboats, but it seemed to be something that was completely beyond the grasp of the people. They could not understand anything that large, nor that they had arrived from beyond the mouth of the fjord.

Jotun? one asked.

That *was* a word he knew, and one that almost brought a laugh. *Jotun* were legendary ice-giants said to dwell in the furthest northern lands.

If I tell them in Ormsdale I was mistaken for a Jotun they will laugh for a week.

He was just about to try to explain that when Tor arrived at his shoulder.

"Skald. We have to go. The snow…"

He brushed Tor off.

"You go ahead. I need more time here. I will be down soon. I promise."

"No," Tor said. "The snow is too heavy. It is either

go now or wait here till the storm has passed. And Per said..."

"Yes," Skald said wearily. "I know what Per said. I'm coming."

If I am to be Viking, I must do as my Captain asks.

He turned, and somehow managed to convey to the inhabitants of the cave that he was leaving, but that he would be back. They watched him, unblinking, until he turned and followed Tor.

He very quickly realised that Tor had been right about the weather. The wind whipped up snow into his face, and threatened to blow him off the path below the skull-rock. He used his staff to lever himself against the wind's force and slowly made his way downwards, following the barely visible figure of Tor ahead of him.

Now that he'd stopped trying to converse with the people in the cave, the memory of the wyrding came back to him once more, made stronger by the sight of the snow whirling around him.

Blood and snow. Drums and doom.

And now he had the memory of the *roar* in his head, not knowing whether it was real, or something that had escaped with him out of the wyrd.

He felt his cloak. It had already stiffened where the Alma's blood had soaked into it. His right arm hurt, and he knew it was because he'd used it, over and over, to thrust a knife into the beast. But he had no memory of it. It was in a black hole inside his mind that he couldn't reach, wasn't sure he wanted to reach.

But with every step down the hill his heartbeat pounded louder, echoing in his head.

He wasn't at all surprised when the roar came again, closer now, from somewhere inside the group of huts. Ahead of him Tor started to run. Skald began to hobble faster, using his staff to try to maintain balance.

Screams rose from the settlement, high pitched

wails of terror.

"Tor," Skald shouted, but his voice was lost in the wind.

Everything was white, a dancing sheet of snow that swirled around him as if alive.

And in the snow, blood. Drops of it at first, like beads of red ice.

Per's dogs barked.

Then came another roar, the fury of a beast.

White turned red and drums beat in his head.

He hobbled forward to the edge of the settlement. He had just reached the first roundhouse when something heavy cracked him on the back of the skull and he fell into darkness.

7

Tor was halfway down the hill when he heard the roar from within the settlement. He looked back, but couldn't see Skald anywhere behind him -- the snow was getting too thick.

But if he is behind me, he will be safe.

Tor hefted his axe and broke into a run, moving as fast as he could through the muddy slush and snow. Somewhere ahead of him a Viking screamed. It was a wail that spoke of pain the likes of which no man should be forced to endure. Tor threw caution to the wind and leaped down the hill.

By the time he arrived at the first hut the sound had stopped and all was quiet.

He stood still, hearing only the pounding of his heart in his ears, the soft hiss of falling snow and the whistle of the wind around the edges of his helm.

The wolfhounds started frenzied barking.

Huginn, Muninn.

Tor ran towards the noise, aware that he was heading back to the same spot where they had killed the first beast.

When he arrived at the East Side of the settlement he almost thought he was dreaming, reliving the earlier scene. A group of Viking stood in a semicircle while the dogs barked and yelped at a white creature cornered at the midden between the two buildings.

But this was no pregnant female. The beast towered above the Viking, half as tall again as the tallest man, near four feet wide across the shoulder with muscles bunched and taut like rocks under the skin. It was snow-white all over apart from on the palms, where the skin was tough and leathery, almost black. Shaggy hair hung around its thighs like a thick kilt that almost reached its knees and it smelled, musky and almost rancid, like a boggy pool after a run of hot days.

The bloody ruined corpse of the female hung from one huge hand, and it cradled one of the mangled foetuses in the other. It ignored the dogs completely, and the dozen Viking arranged around it were unsure what to do next.

Per arrived seconds after Tor.

"Huginn, Muninn. Heel." Per shouted. "Come to heel."

But the dogs had their blood up, and refused to obey, taking turns at trying to run in and nip at the ankles of the beast.

"You men, back to the boats with the rest," Per shouted.

Several of them moved, but Kai and his men stood their ground, spears held towards the beast.

"Kai. Get back to the boat. We are leaving this place."

Kai and his men stepped forward, spears in front of them. Still the beast ignored them.

"You run if you wish Father," Kai said. "But we have a troll to kill here. And this one *shall* be mine."

The beast laid the bloody foetus on the ground, gently, almost reverentially. It stood, head down, stroking the fur of the ruined corpse of the female, then laid her on the ground alongside the foetus.

"Kai," Per said softly. "Step away. You have no idea what you are facing."

Kai laughed.

"It is a beast, and I am Viking. What more do I need to know?"

He walked forward, prodding the tip of a spear towards the beast.

And finally, it turned its attention to him. It stared

straight at him. Huge nostrils flared, steaming slightly in the cold air. It ran a thick red tongue over cold blue lips, then raised the upper lip in semblance of a smile. Its arms hung loosely at its side, but it flexed its fingers, curling and uncurling them. Tor had seen the same action in angry men in their cups in the Great Hall.

He is preparing for a fight.

Tor wasn't the only one to notice.

"Kai," Per said again. "Stand away."

"I am no coward Father," Kai said as he took another step forward. "I at least will not flee."

He has learned nothing from the last time.

The beast watched him come forward. It curled its fingers one last time, and its muscles tensed. But it never took its eyes off Kai or the spear.

Kai prodded the spear at it.

When it moved it was with a speed that surprised every man there. It grabbed the spear and pulled the shaft towards itself. Kai was so surprised that he forgot to let go and was dragged right into the creature's reach. It raised a hand, fingers splayed, nails ready to rip like talons. Kai was struck immobile, unable to do anything but stare at his doom coming for him.

"Kai!" Per shouted, and ran forward, sword raised. The beast turned and swung in one movement, a closed fist smashing the Captain in the side of the head. Only Per's helm saved him from a caved skull, but he fell to the ground, senseless, his sword falling away to one side. The beast stamped a huge white foot down on Per's chest, just once, and the Captain lay still.

Kai scrambled backward on his arse away from the beast and struggled to his feet. He looked at Per's still body and a grim smile played on his lips.

"I am Captain now," he called. "Back to the boats."

The beast raised its head and roared. Kai's henchmen needed no other excuse. They turned and fled. The remainder of the Viking looked down at the Captain and, deciding that discretion was the greater part of valour joined them.

"The Captain may not be dead," Tor said, grabbing at Kai's arm. He was brushed off. "Your *father* may still live."

"He is as good as dead," Kai said. "But if you want to make sure, stay then, and die with him like a good little pet."

Kai left to join the other departing Viking.

Tor stood there with the wolfhounds at his side. The beast stood over Per's unmoving body, like a cat guarding a recently caught mouse. Tor stepped forward and showed the beast his axe, but it just looked at him from those pale milky eyes.

Tor didn't want to press an attack, but the Captain still hadn't moved, and might need help urgently. The beast curled and uncurled its fingers again.

It wants a fight. It enjoys the battle.

But it showed no sign of being impetuous, and seemed happy to wait for him to make the first move.

The dogs decided matters for him. They snarled, and pounced in attack at the same time.

Huginn died almost immediately. It leaped for the throat as it had been trained. The snow-beast caught the dog in mid air, heaved the closing jaws away from its throat and threw the dog away. Huginn smashed against the wall of a hut with so much force that his ribs burst in broken pieces from the chest. The dog fell to the ground in a pile of broken bone and torn flesh, leaving a bloody stain on the wall.

The death wasn't completely in vain.

Muninn leapt and latched its teeth in the beast's throat, at the same time tearing and scratching at the torso with the claws on its rear legs. The time it took the beast to grab the dog gave Tor the opportunity to step in and wield the axe. He swung it sideways, as if chopping at a tree. He embedded the blade deep in the beast's side, so deep that the blade grated against bone. He tugged, trying to release the weapon, but it was stuck fast, and when the beast spun round towards him it dragged the handle from his hand, taking skin that had been frozen there with it.

Tor rolled away, turning just in time to see Muninn be torn to pieces, ripped apart like a piece of wet cloth. Its insides became its outside and red guts fell with a splash in the snow at the creature's feet.

The beast pulled the axe from its side. Blood flowed. It raised its head and bellowed in pain. The noise was so great as to shake fresh snow from the roofs of the nearby huts. It held the axe in one great hand, studying it, then threw it aside.

Its pale gaze fell on Tor again.

It opened its mouth, showing long yellow teeth, the top canine broken in a ragged stump. The red tongue rolled like a lump of meat as it roared in the wind. Once again Tor smelled old fish.

It showed him its smile again as it came for him.

Tor's hand touched cold metal as he rolled away, and he grabbed for it in desperation. When he stood, it was with Per's long sword in his hand.

The beast came on, roaring worse than any thunderstorm, the wind at its back whipping snow into Tor's eyes. He could do little but raise the sword and brace himself. It hit him so hard that he was thrown back against the stone wall of one of the houses. Pain flared in his back and the full weight of the beast fell on top of him as both of them crumpled to the ground. The stench so close up made him gag, and all he could see was a wall of muck-caked fur. He fought, trying to release the sword. The weight was too much and he was trapped. The beast brought its face up and looked straight into his eyes. It opened its mouth and dripped a heavy rope of drool down onto Tor's chest.

And now I die.

Tor composed himself for the inevitable end, but the weight suddenly lifted away, and the beast whimpered. Tor tried to stand. The whole length of the sword was red with the beast's blood.

I have caused it pain.

He used the sword to push himself upright. The beast stood near Per, holding a hand to a deep wound in its left shoulder. Blood poured both there, and from the axe wound in its side.

Tor stepped forward and showed it the sword again.

It roared at him, but it did not have the same strength in it as previously. It bent, lifted the corpse of the female, and bounded away, lost in the snow in seconds.

Tor considered following, but a weak voice from below made him look down.

"A fine blow lad," Per said. He coughed, and blood gushed down his beard as he tried to get to his knees. He groaned, and went white as pain hit him.

Tor helped him up, and Per managed to stand, leaning heavily on Tor's shoulder.

"It is gone?" he asked.

Tor nodded.

"For now at least. I cut it with the axe, a blow that would fell a good-sized tree. And still it came at me. I would not like to face its like again."

Per laughed. "Nor would I lad. Nor would I."

More blood came up.

"Busted inside somewhere," he said. "It had heavy feet."

Tor made to hand him the sword.

"No lad," the Captain said. "You carry it for a while.

I doubt I have the strength. Get me to the boat."

In lieu of the sword, Tor passed his axe to Per as something to lean on. Together they hobbled through the huddle of roundhouses.

It was only then that Tor though of Skald. He realised there had been no sign of his friend since they'd parted on the hill.

He's probably still there, Tor thought. *Practising his mummery.*

The snow was thicker now, and the wind picked up, howling around his ears and throwing biting cold onto his face. He tried to look towards the hill where he'd left Skald, but all was white.

"The boat it is," he whispered. "But I'll be back soon."

As they left the scene of the fight Tor saw Per look back at the broken shells that had once been the wolfhounds.

If there was a tear in the Captain's eye as they made for the shore, Tor chose to put it down to the pain.

8

Skald was lost somewhere deep within the wyrd.

He lay on his back amongst a sea of rustling grass as silken cloud wafted across an azure blue sky. It felt like he had lain in this spot forever. Indeed he had no thought of moving, not on so beautiful a day.

There are no drums.

Part of him was aware that the wyrd was showing him something new, a place he had never before been. Another part, a large part, did not care, being content to lie and watch the clouds make patterns that *almost* resolved into faces.

He lay there for a long time. What finally got him moving was his curiosity.

The wyrd has never done anything without a reason. It seems I must discover what that reason is.

He looked around for his staff, but it was nowhere to be seen. He pushed himself upright with both arms, and winced in anticipation of pain to follow.

But it did not come. Both of his legs worked as they had before the accident, and he walked across a lush green meadow with confident strides. The sun felt warm on his face and the air smelled of summer flowers. The soft buzz of bees was the only noise on the windless morning.

Skald felt alive. More than that, he knew he was in the wyrd, and knew that *this* was the natural order of things.

This is truth.

If Valhalla was anywhere it was in some section of the wyrd, of that he was certain.

Maybe this is my Valhalla, he thought. *I may be no warrior, but surely I will get some measure of peace?*

The meadow seemed to go on forever, but Skald

had nothing else he needed to be doing that was of any import. He wandered, watching the bees, running his hands through the grasses.

He'd been hearing it for some time before he realised there was someone singing in the distance, a high floating lay that he *almost* recognised. He walked towards the song, cresting a small hill and looked down.

An old woman sat on a long flat stone by a languid river. Despite the heat of the sun, she wore thick furs that covered her from head to toe. As Skald approached she lowered the hood. She was almost bald and as Skald got closer he saw that her whole head -- scalp, ears and all, was covered in tiny tattoos.

Never breaking from the song, she smiled and slapped on the rock beside her to indicate he should sit.

He sat down, cross-legged on the stone.

The first time I have done that without pain since the rock gave way under me.

And still the old woman sang.

After a time Skald began to recognise patterns in the song, and a while after that he started to understand.

It was her telling.

Before the snow came there was only stone.

And the stone was alone, in the blackness, even before the light, even before any songs were written. The stone desired company, but there was only cold and dark and empty. And the stone cried.

Where the stone tears fell, they dug holes in the firmament of the night. And silver and blue fire came from the holes, a fire that blazed in the heavens and gladdened the cold heart of the stone. And so the stars were formed.

The stone sang to itself in the dark, and the stars

came to listen. And the stone loved the stars so that he sent out to them for one to come closer, to warm him there in the dark.

And one came close, to better hear the song of the stone. And they sang to each other, the stone and the star. The star warmed the stone, and the stone cooled the ardour of the star. And from their love they made the world of light and stone together. And they brought forth the land and the seas. And they made a song to care for their creation. And he was the first, their son, our Father.

And there in the earth our Father grew strong in the love of the stone and the stars. But as he grew, he too became lonely. And he sang to the sun, and he sang to the stone, but they have their own song, one that he could not sing.

So the Father taught himself new music, tunes that made the earth move and give forth trees and herbs, fish and fowl. But still the Father was lonely, for although he loved his creations, none of them could sing for him.

So the Father took the sound of waves crashing on beaches and wind blowing through trees. And he took the whistles from the birds and the barking cough from the dogs. And from the cats he took the crying wail, and from the wolf, the Grey Shadow, he took the howl in the night. All these noises he took, and he blew them into the stone, and mixed them with tears from his own loneliness.

And for a whole tour of the earth round the sun he moulded the stone with his tears, and in the moulding he added the new song he had found. And slowly we his children were born, and our song with us.

In the stone we were held with the Father, and our souls were empty. And we were one with the stone and the stone was one with us. And so it went for long aeons. The Father told us tales of his youth, when even the stars were young, and he made us promises that we would always be with him.

But there came the day that the wind God came in a great rush, and with her she brought the great ice. The ice covered the whole world, so that even the Father was not safe from its ravages. And the ice leeched into us and through us and separated us from the stone. For the first time we were parted from the Father, and we stood alone before the force of the wind.

And the wind took us and blew us apart like pebbles in a stream until our people were scattered far from the Father and our souls were filled with fear.

And still the wind blew and still our people were tossed and turned this way and that, until we came at last to rest in this place.

For long years the wind blew and the ice grew, and many perished, but there came a time when the wind began to lessen. And in the darkness, as the wind abated, we could hear the cries of our Father, but we could not come to him, for he was locked deep in the ice, in a place we could not reach.

So we gathered and we made slaves for the digging, strong beasts that would do our bidding in our quest to return the Father's glory. Deep we delved, and our songs brought warmth to him, there under the icy mountain. But still we could not come to him.

And in our rush to reach him, we lost sight of ourselves. We made the beasts too well. They grew strong, and moved as fast as the wind itself. And they caught the slowest of us, and took them from the Father so that their songs had gone in the wind forever.

Slowly we learned how to fight them, and we learned how to kill, but every time we killed, or were killed, our souls became a little more full, and we became a little further from the Father.

Until there came a day when we could no longer hear the Father, and our warmth no longer reached him. And our people met in the place of the digging, and decided that we would kill no more, but neither would we allow the shadows to take us.

So we took ourselves out of the sight of the shadows, away from the place of the digging and after a time our songs began to warm the Father once more.

Since then we have walked with the wind.

But now the day has come. You have come from the north to lead us back to the place of the digging, where we will once more be one with the Father.

To prepare for that day we empty our souls, and we keep to the old ways and we sing our songs. We do this in the sure and certain knowledge that our time has come again and soon our Father will have us back there with him, in the place of the digging, in the bosom of the stone.

The song stopped. The old woman smiled again, and rapped him hard on the forehead with her knuckles.

You have come from the north to lead us back to the place of the digging, where we will once more be one with the Father.

Skald woke up, and tears formed in his eyes.

He was back in the world of pain.

9

By the time Tor and Per reached the water's edge they could barely see five yards ahead of them. The ships were little more than looming shadows in the snow. Tor guessed that night was falling, as the darkness had closed in fast.

Indeed, even as he thought it, a firebrand was lit in the brow of the nearest ship.

"Hello on board," he called as he waded through the freezing water. "Our Captain needs aid."

"The Captain? He lives?"

"Only if you let me out of this fucking water," Per called, and doubled over, coughing up more blood. Tor bent to help, but Per pushed himself upright.

"I must make it on my own from here," he said to Tor. "Give me back the sword. I must stand tall. No weakness can be shown."

Tor passed the tall sword back, and Per managed a grim smile as he leaned on it.

"My thanks lad. And if I falter, it is good to know that such as you has my back."

He handed the axe back to Tor.

"Once aboard, you may have need of this sooner than you think. Kai may have set them against me. If that be the case, then things might not go well for us."

Tor hefted the axe.

"I have faced far worse this day already. I'm your man."

Per laughed and clasped Tor on the arm.

"We have made you Viking already lad. Your father would have been proud."

"Father?" Kai said from above them, and, bending over, reached out a hand. "We thought you lost."

Per ignored the hand and reached up over the keel.

He managed to haul himself on board the *Drakenskin* but as he looked back at Tor he was grey with pain after the effort. Tor pulled himself aboard beside the Captain, and was just in time to see a smile disappear from Kai's face.

"What is wrong," Per said. "Did you hope I was dead? Or did you really run off to get more men? If so, you are a mite tardy."

"Father, I..."

"Do not speak to me," Per said. "Get to work. We need to make shelter, for this storm is about to get worse."

"I have given orders to make sail," Kai said.

Per laughed.

"In this? You really *are* as stupid as you look. Cover the decks and make ready for wind. It is going to be a long hard night."

Kai stepped forward, hand on sword. Tor moved to Per's shoulder. Kai looked him up and down.

"I see your *pet* survived," Kai said.

Per spat a wad of blood at Kai's feet.

"This *man* fought off yon beast and saved your Captain's life," Per said. "What did you do? You poked it with a sharp stick then ran away. Here Tor, take this. You have carried it with honour already. Now it is yours by right."

Per handed his sword to Tor. Tor had to put the axe down to take it, but the Captain's weapon sat in his palm like an old friend's handshake. He swung it in the air twice, testing its weight, then held it by his side, relaxed, but ready if need be.

Kai's eyes grew wide, and anger was close to flaring in him, but he stepped back, holding his tongue. Tor swung the sword again, and smiled.

An older Viking stepped forward.

"Captain? It is good to see you still with us. Kai had

you slaughtered and disembowelled by a troll."

"Kai has brains and courage in equal measure," Per said, and hawked up more bloody sputum.

Kai spun on his heels and left them.

"He has you making sail?" Per asked the older Viking.

"That was the order," the sail-master said. "But I have held off, in hope of your return. Shall we pull up on the shore?"

Per checked the wind.

"No time master Bjorn. Lash the boats together at anchor, get the sails down and over the decks, and pray that Thor's anger will pass us by. It is going to be a long night."

The sail-master left them, barking orders at Viking along the length of the longboat, and Per once more leaned on Tor's shoulder.

"Come lad," he said. "I'll need some help getting this helm off. I almost fear to move it lest it is the only thing keeping my brains in my head."

Per was right about the weather. The Viking on all three ships had to fight the wind and snow to make their sails into rough tents over their keels. By the time they hunkered down under the makeshift shelters the gale was blowing the snow horizontally across their bows, shrieking like a tortured cat as it did so. The tarpaulins flapped and strained at the ropes, but they were holding, for now.

Tor sat at the stern in the small tent covered in furs that served as the Captain's private bedding area. Per lay on a straw mattress, looking as dead as Skald had on the night of his accident. Tor held the man's hand. The Captain was alternating between bouts of fevered sleep and moments of wakening. Tor leaned forward as his eyes fluttered.

"Are we protected?" Per asked.

Bubbles of blood burst on his lips as Tor nodded.

"The boats are lashed together, the anchors are loose enough that we will not batter each other to kindling, and the sails are slung. We are as safe as we can be, for a while. But Kai is not happy."

Per tried to laugh, but it was too much effort, and more blood came, at lips and nose. Tor wiped it away with a wet cloth as Per struggled to speak.

"Kai hasn't been happy since I skelped his arse to ensure his first breath."

He grasped Tor's hand tight.

"Be careful with him lad. When I'm gone, he must be Captain -- that is our way. But the sword is yours. You earned it today. Do not let him take it from you."

Per sat partially upright.

"You must not strain yourself," Tor said, pushing against the Captain's chest to try to get him to lie down. Per pushed him away roughly.

"I am not going anywhere... even if I should want to. I just want to give you this."

He unbuckled his thick leather scabbard. It was intricately worked with knot-work and beading showing a sea-wyrm being netted from a longboat. It had been at the man's waist for as long as Tor could remember.

"Wear this. My Elfrida made it for me many summers ago, and it would gladden my heart to see it pass to a warrior before I go."

"Hush," Tor said, taking the scabbard and pushing the man back down on the mattress. "You said it yourself. You are not going anywhere."

Per smiled.

"This will be my last Viking lad. The halls of Asgard await my coming. I can already hear the drinking songs of Valhalla," he said. "And I shall be there by morning. I will tell your father that he sired a fine man, and my old friend and I will share much mead, and many women."

Tor looked at the scabbard in his hand.

"This too should go to Kai," he said.

"No," Per said, almost a whisper. "It goes to a man worthy of carrying it. The son I should have had."

He gripped tight at Tor's forearm, then released the pressure. When Tor looked down, Per had fallen into sleep, a smile on his face even despite the blood that oozed around his lips with every breath.

Tor buckled on the scabbard and sheathed the sword. The weight of it swinging at his waist felt natural as he pulled back the flap of cloth and stepped out to the deck. He had to stoop, so he almost didn't notice that someone was huddled there in front of him.

"You are carrying my sword," Kai said, having to shout to be heard above the wind.

"No," Tor replied. "I am carrying your father's sword. You have your own on your hip."

Kai stepped in front of him.

"You will give it to me now,"

Tor stared back. He realised that he looked eye to eye with the other man, for the first time in their lives. Kai was elder, by near a year, and had made Tor's younger life a misery.

But no more.

Tor stood silent. Kai put his hand on the hilt of his sword and still Tor didn't move.

"It is mine by right," Kai said.

Tor knew then that he had him. Kai had allowed a whining query to creep into his voice, and looked away as Tor took a step forward.

"Your father is sleeping," Tor said and pushed his way past the man. "I would not wake him unduly... he has my axe by his side, and in his fever might mistake you for someone else.

Someone a bit more Viking.

Tor left him there and went in search of food. Wind and snow beat against the makeshift tent in irregular drumbeats and crept under the ropes to chill all exposed flesh to the bone. Most of the crew sat huddled around a small brazier, drinking a hot brew of hazel tea and mead.

"Sit lad," the sail-master said. "And have some of this. It will not keep the cold at bay, but it will make you feel a lot better about it."

Several of the crew watched Tor as he poured himself a beaker, but no one spoke as he sat beside them. He drank in silence, listening to the wind howl. Now that he had stopped tending to the Captain, he had time to worry about other matters.

He still had the smell of the beast on him.

The stench of it might never leave me.

It had been wounded, and was now out there, somewhere in the snow beyond the village. Tor had enough experience of wolf and bear to know that a wounded beast could prove a lot more trouble than a healthy one. And Skald was also somewhere out there, with no fellow Viking to stand by his side should the beast come upon him in the storm.

Skald. Where are you?

Tor had considered heading ashore to search for Skald, but when he'd raised his head above the prow the wind almost knocked him backwards and the snow blinded him within seconds. When he got back to the brazier it was to find ice melting from his helm.

"Stay close lad," Bjorn said. "It is on such nights that the wild hunt goes by, and *that's* a sight you do not want to see."

Tor sat, and drank more of the mead than was good for him; thankful for the heat it spread in his stomach.

Bjorn the sail-master was first to voice what many of them were thinking.

"What *was* that thing? I have seen much, and travelled far, but that was something I have never even *heard* of."

The older Viking around the brazier nodded in agreement.

"It is something from the old days," one said. "A bastard child of Loki?"

"They are certainly ugly enough. I will ne'er forget the way they just *tore* those men apart, like they were no more than corn dolls."

They all fell silent again, staring into the brazier, remembering.

"Kai said they were trolls," Tor said.

"Kai says a lot of things," one of them replied softly. "Nary a one of them worth listening to."

There were some nods of agreement round the brazier, but none spoke too loudly. For the first time, Tor realised that Kai was not well liked.

They fell quiet again, and more mead was drunk, so much so that Tor started to feel light in the head. He put the beaker down.

"It was no kind of troll I have ever heard tell of," Bjorn said after a time. "I heard tell that trolls are bald, with skin like grey stone. Not white as death and as hairy as Ragnar's breeks."

"We killed a troll in Orkney three summers ago," another said. "It looked nothing like that."

"That is because what you killed was a fat, drunk Scotsman," Bjorn said, and the men laughed, but only for a second. The wind quickly took their humour away.

"There was a tale I once heard, from a Captain who went further south than any Viking afore him," Bjorn said. "I heard it from his son's son. Nobody believed him, but he told of a high rocky island in a narrow inlet to the great sea that leads to Rome and Greece. And on that island, small hairy men frolicked and played. 'Tis said they were vicious when roused. Mayhap what Tor and the Captain fought today was like them?"

"It was vicious enough, that's for certain" Tor said. "But it was far from small."

He missed Bjorn's reply. He was thinking of something else, of the tenderness the beast had shown for the dead female.

That was not the action of a wild animal. It may be much more like us than we yet know.

He kept that thought to himself. It was not something the others needed to hear

"Tell me, what happened with the Captain?" Bjorn said, leaning in to speak in Tor's ear. "Did he kill the male?"

Tor looked up the boat before answering. Kai and his men hung around the Captain's area, but Tor noted with a grim smile that they seemed afraid to venture inside.

Tor told his tale to Bjorn, and the older man nodded and clapped Tor on the back.

"You have made some enemies this day," the sail-master said. "But also many friends. Remember that... when the time comes."

10

Skald opened his eyes and looked up into the smiling round face of the old woman.

At first he thought he might still be in the wyrd, but as his eyes came into focus he saw the stone roof of a cave overhead. Wind whistled around them, but he found that he was quite warm. He tried to sit up, and had to struggle through several layers of thick clothing. He had been swaddled in heavy furs. They smelled as if they'd been rolled in damp shit then pissed on, and even breathing through his mouth didn't help much, but when he took a layer off his shoulders he immediately felt the cold bite, and quickly covered himself up.

The rock overhead glistened damply, and red shadows cast sharply against the walls from burning firebrands that added a thick black smoke to the already cloying intensity of the smells.

I will never complain about the smell of Per's farts again.

There was a muted murmur of talk in the room, in a guttural language he felt he could *almost* understand. Just by looking in his immediate vicinity, he saw there were more than thirty of the small people huddled together, adults and children, all staring at him, unblinking.

I'm an enigma to them. Like the troll was to us, so we are to these.

The old woman smiled again, and rapped him on the forehead. His head rang in pain. Feeling the back of his skull he found a tender lump the size of a hen's egg.

"Who hit me?" he said.

She covered her ears with her hands, then covered her mouth.

She cannot understand me. Not outside the wyrd.

"Back to the mummery then," he said to himself.

It was much simpler than earlier. The old woman, who Skald soon learned was called Baren, was adept at picking up small nuances, and Skald suspected the wyrd was helping matters more than a little.

Once more Skald tried to tell of the Viking, and their coming in the longboats, and this time Baren understood. But still she insisted that it had been foretold. The old woman rapped him hard on the forehead with her knuckles again, and he heard the voice from the earlier wyrding.

You have come from the north to lead us back to the place of the digging, where we will once more be one with the father.

She handed him a small amulet on a leather thong. It was a piece of intricate knot-work, done in solid silver, and Skald knew immediately that the metal was a by-product of their digging long ago in their history. It was not the main reason they dug, for that was to try to reach their *Father*. But the silver reminded them that the *Father* was there, waiting for them.

It is a symbol of hope.

Skald handed it back, but she refused to take it, indicating that it was a gift, for him.

He thanked her with a kiss on her cheek that made her blush like a girl. He put the amulet over his head and hid it away under the folds of fur.

She put out a hand and invited him to stand. When he did so he was surprised to see that she barely reached as high as his chest. She handed him his staff, and together they hobbled to one wall of the cave. She took a firebrand and motioned him towards the wall. Inscribed there, and gleaming in red relief in the flickering light, was the story of her people, laid out on the stone as he'd been told it in the wyrd.

She walked him along it to the end. There it showed a representation of a tall mountain. High on its flanks an entrance led down to a cave system where deep mines plunged deeper still into the roots of the hill and a vast temple was carved out of a high cavern.

All around that temple the hairy figures of the *Alma* danced.

Tens... nay, hundreds of them.

11

The storm howled.

Several times the crew had to be organised to move the snow that accumulated on the sail above and threatened to collapse it atop them. And several times Tor went to check on the Captain. Per still slept, but it was a nervous, feverish sleep that had taken him, and underneath the furs the man burned from within with a heat like a summer sun.

On one of his trips Bjorn the sail-master accompanied him. His face was pained when he rose from attending to the Captain.

"He will be gone by morning," he said. "Something is seriously broken in him."

Tor nodded.

"That is what he said. But he managed to walk from the settlement to the boat. There may be hope yet."

Bjorn said nothing. He didn't have to. His face told Tor just how little hope there was.

Bjorn looked down at the sleeping man.

"He has been my Captain on eight Viking," he said. "And never have I seen a better man. He will be a sore loss. All the more so when I contemplate who will take his place."

"Kai?"

Bjorn spat.

"Aye. Kai. He showed me again today that he is a fool. But worse than that, he has no stomach for a real fight. He is no Viking. Not at heart, where it counts."

"What can be done?" Tor asked.

Bjorn sighed.

"Done? Nothing can be done. Kai is his father's son, and will be Captain. That is our way."

But it doesn't mean we have to like it.

Tor went back to the brazier. Kai hadn't taken his eyes from the sword all night.

Sometime soon him and I are going to have a serious problem.

But Tor did not have time to worry about Kai. His mind was too full of thoughts of the Captain and worry for Skald. He hoped against hope for a break in the storm.

For if I cannot help Per, surely I can find my friend, and bring him back to his kinsmen.

But the storm showed no signs of abating. Indeed, the wind strengthened a notch, and the ropes holding the sails stretched and complained. The crew huddled ever closer together around the brazier as an endless supply of the hazel tea and mead was warmed and passed around.

Tar Karlsson was first to move, for he had taken more mead than any other, and had not moved from the brazier since they'd come back aboard.

"I need to go, for I shall pish my breeks if I do not," he said, standing.

"I have pished mine twice already," Bjorn called. "That is what keeps me warm."

Tar headed for the leeward side and started to fumble in his folds of clothing.

"Do not take it out for too long," Bjorn shouted after him. "It might freeze and drop off."

"How would he tell the difference?" another called out.

They were still laughing when the white arm came out of the snow, grabbed Tar Karlsson by the legs, and dragged him overboard. His head hit the stern, hard, on the way over, and then he was lost in the night, leaving only a bloody smear to show where he had stood.

The Viking didn't move for a second, stunned into

silence. Then a scream came from the *Windmaister* on their port side, one that was quickly cut off.

Tor stood and unsheathed his sword while the rest of the Viking grabbed for weapons. Along the length of the boat, men were roused from slumber and came groggily awake. They stood in rough circles, watching each other's backs as they had been taught from childhood. There was no sound but the rush of wind and the flapping of the tarpaulin above them.

Another scream rent the air from the *Windmaister*.

"In Odin's name, help us," a lone voice cried in the storm.

Tor would have gone to their aid, but Bjorn held him back.

"Stand with us lad," Bjorn said. "I fear we shall have perils of our own to deal with afore long."

Bjorn was right.

A white hand came over the saxboard and tore loose two of the rings holding the sail in place. The wind immediately grabbed the tarpaulin and took it flapping off into the night. At the same time a beast hauled itself up onto the boat and roared. Tor only had time to notice that this one had no wounds on its body before it leaped across the deck.

Snow threatened to blind him. Icy flakes bit at Tor's face like summer insects, but he couldn't take his eyes from the beast. It was as large as the one he'd fought off earlier, but this one had come prepared for a fight. It stood straight and pounded at its chest with the palms of its hands, raised its face to the sky and roared into the wind, giving them all a clear view of four-inch teeth that looked as sharp as razors.

It fell forward into a hunch, and threw itself at them. The three men facing it hefted their spears, putting their feet on them and standing firm as the weight hit and rocked them backward. One spear went through the beast's right shoulder but didn't slow it. It broke the shaft and thrust the broken end straight back at its wielder, going in through the Viking's mouth and out the back of his skull with a sudden spray of blood and brain and bone.

A second beast jumped aboard further down the boat, swinging from the mainmast and barrelling feet first into a knot of men, knocking then flying. Bones cracked, loud even above the howl of the wind, and screams rent the air.

More screams came from their sister ships, and suddenly the night was full of bloody carnage and the raging howls of beasts.

In Odin's name, how many are there?

Then Tor was too busy himself to pay attention to the fighting elsewhere, as a beast came over the side coming straight at him.

He raised the sword.

The beast eyed it warily.

They have learned quickly.

This one was smaller than the other, but still towered several inches taller than Tor. It showed Tor its teeth as it smiled, then roared its defiance, but it stayed out of reach of the sword, never taking its eyes off the weapon. Tor feinted towards it, and it moved to one side.

"Tor," Bjorn shouted behind him. "We need you round here."

From the corner of his eye Tor saw the first beast was on its knees. Three dead Viking lay around it. Three more, Bjorn included, were trying to get inside its reach to deliver a killing blow.

Tor did not speak. He knew that if he took his eye off the beast, even for a second, it would be on him. It swayed, moving from side to side, still watching the sword.

More screams came from behind Tor, and the roars of the beasts grew louder.

"Viking. To me," came the shout.

Per?

Tor made an almost fatal mistake. He looked towards the Captain's call.

The beast jumped, coming straight for Tor, its legs clear of the deck. Tor's instincts kicked in and he fell backwards and sideways into a roll that brought him up at the creature's side even as its leap was taking it past him. He brought the sword overhead in a high swing, and down on the back of the beast's neck. Warm blood splashed his face as the head almost parted from the torso. The beast fell with a heavy thud on the deck.

Tor remembered to breathe.

"Viking. To me," came the shout again.

Bjorn and the others had managed to subdue the first beast, and the huge corpse lay on the deck next to the bodies of the Viking it had slain.

The knot of men around the mast had not been so successful. One of the beasts stomped through a pile of bodies, bloody gore splattered all the way up its legs to its hips. As Tor watched it bent and opened a man's rib cage just by thrusting its hands into his chest. The man screamed and his feet drummed a manic rhythm on the deck as his ribs were splayed like wings. Thankfully, he quickly fell silent.

The beast smeared blood over its face as it ate his heart.

Beyond the feeding beast Per stood alone at the far end of the boat. He held two of the beasts at bay with burning firebrands in each hand.

"Captain!" Tor called, and started to run.

12

Baren handed Skald the leather pouch that contained his wyrding bones. She made a movement, indicating casting, then pointed at him.

She wants a telling.

Skald felt weak, almost to the point of slipping into a senseless sleep. The wyrd had called him too much, with too little rest.

I'm not sure I can do this.

He hefted the pouch in his hand.

Baren again made the casting motion. Skald sighed, opened the pouch, and cast the bones on the floor. Almost immediately the wyrding came on him.

It started the same as before, with the drums.

They beat, slowly at first, then in an ever-increasing frenzy until his skull threatened to split apart. Behind the drums, wind howled, a raging shriek that grew higher and higher.

Everything was white, a dancing sheet of snow that swirled around him as if alive.

And in the snow, blood. Drops of it at first, like beads of red ice.

Then came a roar.

White turned red as the drums beat a word into his skull.

Doom.

Even deep in the wyrd, Skald knew that this was the end of it, that soon he would reawaken. But this time proved to be a surprise, and not a pleasant one.

The snow cleared.

Twenty fur-clad figures moved across an ice field, battling through a gale. All twenty looked as miserable as any men who ever lived. Cold gripped them, turning their faces almost blue and caking their beards with a thick layer of ice.

Snow fell again, obscuring the scene.

He was in a huge echoing cavern filled with a dim light that seemed to come from the very walls itself. Two tall columns of black stone dominated the far end. Behind them seemingly carved straight into the rock wall, was a massive plinth, on which lay a giant effigy of a bound figure, mouth wide open, screaming for eternity. Alma, dozens of them, carried screaming Viking through the chamber and slung their bodies onto the plinth. They tore open the still living bodies, coolly methodically, disembowelling tearing. Blood splattered on and around the plinth...but most ran down the runnels towards the statue. And where the blood hit it, the stone began to change, lightening in colour, softening, as it took on the texture of hair and flesh, soaking up the blood, drinking it in.

Then came a roar.

White turned red as the drums beat a word into his skull.

Doom.

Skald blinked and woke. His head span and his body felt so light that the slightest breeze might blow him away.

The old woman rapped him hard on the forehead with her knuckles again, and once again he heard the voice from the wyrding.

You have come from the north to lead us back to the place of the digging, where we will once more be one with the father.

Skald was very afraid that he now knew what that father might be.

13

Even as Tor started running, the bloodied beast stood away from the pile of bodies and stepped into his path.

Tor barely noticed it. A backhanded downward cut cleaved its left arm off at the shoulder, and while the beast looked at the wound in puzzlement a second cut drove down on the right side of its head at the neck, opening a wound down through the chest. By the time the body hit the deck Tor was already halfway towards Per.

A knot of men stood in the centre of the boat holding off three of the beasts, but Tor did not stop to aid them. He slashed, hard, at the back of a beast in passing, bringing a howl of pain and a splash of blood. It gave one of the defenders the opportunity to drive a spear through the beast's neck. Blood flew in the air to join the snow as Tor leapt along the deck, sword raised above his head.

The closest beast somehow sensed his approach and turned, just as Tor brought the sword down in a chopping cut that bit deep into its ribs. It wailed and roared, tearing the sword from its side and spraying hot blood over Tor's face as it leaped for him. Tor feinted, stepped to one side, and took its head off with one smooth cut. He turned back to help Per with the other, but the older man had already thrust both firebrands into the creature's face. Its mane caught, and the air filled with the stench of burning hair. The beast danced around, flapping its hands at its head and screeching before Tor finally put it out of its misery with a thrust to its heart.

It fell, smouldering, at the Captain's feet.

"Well met lad," Per said.

Tor saw with dismay that blood came to the

Captain's lips with every word, and that the man was near as white as the beast he had just slain.

It is a wonder he can even stand.

"Have you seen Kai?" Per asked.

"No," Tor replied, and smiled. "But I have been a mite busy."

Bjorn the sail-master joined them. He held a cut off oar in his hands, wielded like an axe. Blood, matted hair and brains dripped from its edge. The three men looked down the length of the longboat.

The snow was so thick that the full length of the deck was only just visible, but it was enough to tell Tor that they were in serious trouble. Bodies of slain Viking and beasts lay strewn among a pool of blood and gore... more of the men than of the beasts. A knot of men had gathered around the main mast, ten or more of them armed with spears, tying to hold off six creatures. Kai was behind them inside the ring, sword raised, his face pulled tight with fear. From the windward side came the roars of beasts and the screams of the dying on their sister boats.

"Do we have a plan Captain?" Bjorn said.

Per looked grim.

"Aye. But you're not going to like it. Fetch up the oil."

Bjorn looked the Captain in the eye.

"All of it?"

Per nodded.

"And make it quick. A few more of these beasts and we will all be in Valhalla within the hour... if we are not on the way there already."

Bjorn opened the hatch and went below. Tor joined him in the below-deck area.

"What does he have in mind?" Tor asked.

"A true Viking burial," Bjorn said. His eyes were moist with tears. "And we will give him it. A Viking death, and a Viking burial. Here. Get these up top."

Between them they manhandled two barrels of thick whale oil onto the deck at the Captain's side. Per uncorked them and kicked them over. The oil started to flow down the length of the deck.

Finally Tor saw the plan.

"Viking. To me," Per shouted, raising the firebrands high.

The knot of men around the sail tracked backwards, keeping their spears ever between themselves and the beasts that followed them. Per stepped towards them, feet splashing in the spilled oil.

"Get behind me," he called. "And be ready to jump."

Tor noticed with a grim smile that Kai was first to obey.

"Captain," Tor called out, looking straight at Kai. "If you need a *man* to stand with you, I will be proud of the honour."

Per turned, a grim smile on his red lips.

"Nay lad," he replied. "Your father would never forgive me. But come, I have a last gift for you."

He shucked off his wolf-skin cloak and passed it to Tor.

"I have no more need of it. I shall be warm enough."

Once more Tor saw Kai's eyes flare in rage, but the man said nothing as Tor took the cloak and fastened it with a clasp at his neck over the top of his own.

"Now step back lad, and make ready."

The last of the Viking backed towards Per. Five beasts followed, and Tor saw they were already trampling in the spilled oil.

"We cannot leave you," Tor said. Other Viking had already made their escape over the side, Kai among them.

"You must," Per replied. "Someone will have to keep the men together. Kai doesn't have it in him. Keep them together, and bring them safe home to Ormsdale. For me?"

Tor nodded, but couldn't speak lest tears came.

Now there was only Tor and the sail-master left with the Captain, and the creatures, emboldened, came forward faster.

"Now," Per shouted, and thrust a firebrand down into the oil at his feet. Flame burst along the deck and the creatures erupted in flame.

Tor and Bjorn leaped, and hit the water at the same instant. Tor turned, just in time to see Per, little more than a ball of flame, walk among the beasts, touching them with his fire.

The wind blew snow in his eyes, and when he looked again, the whole length of the boat was aflame. The beasts howled like the raging wind as they died. The skin on Tor's face tightened in the heat but he stood there, thigh deep in the cold water, long after all movement stopped on the longboat deck and the fire took hold along the whole length of the vessel.

14

Skald was once more drawn to the frieze on the long wall. This time he looked back along its length, starting at the carving of the Great Temple and working his way backwards. He had to drag his gaze away from the drawing of the bound giant. There was something about it that disturbed him, but he couldn't yet bring to mind what it was.

Besides, there was much to exercise his imagination elsewhere on the frieze.

He looked closely at the *Alma.* They had been meticulously rendered in miniature, and even the drawings made Skald shiver.

Doom.

Further down the vast picture he found a forested path that led up to the mountains. Here was represented a battle from a time long past, when the *Alma* had risen up against their makers and cast them out of the Temple. Tracing the path backwards brought him across a glacial plane riven with huge cracks. The picture showed small fur clad people dragging their belongings across the ice, all the while being pursued by the *Alma.*

And finally he came to the settlement itself. The picture showed the small people building it while, in the hills above, *Alma* watched.

Baren came and took his hand. She pointed at the *Alma*, then at a firebrand, and then back at a small drawing of one of the beasts rearing away from a flame.

Skald nodded.

Fire. They fear fire.

There was a commotion at the mouth of the cave,

and another of the small people came forward and dragged Skald outside. The cold and the snow immediately bit at his face, but he could just make out what had the people so excited.

Down below, an orange glow showed, even through the snowstorm, and distant wails of pain could be heard in the wind.

Tor.

Skald grabbed a firebrand in one hand, his staff in another, and headed for the path. The small people, similarly armed with brands, followed behind in a line snaking down the hill like a fire-wyrm.

The orange glow got steadily brighter as they descended, but the only noise that Skald could now hear was the whistling of the wind. Snow coated his cheeks and the going underfoot was treacherous, but the thought of what might have happened below was too much to bear and Skald threw himself in a headlong rush down the hill, skidding and sliding all the way.

By the time he arrived at the edge of the settlement the whole of the far side of the town seemed to be lit in red and orange flickering. Dark shadows ran between the buildings, but there was no sign of any *Alma.* Not even a footprint.

Skald was aware that the small people had gathered behind him in a tight bunch. Baren came forward and stood at his side as they walked through the settlement.

The first thing that Skald saw when they reached the shore was the burning wreckage that had once been three longboats. Flames reached high into the air, despite the snow and wind, and the noise of wood snapping in the heat sent out loud cracks.

A group of Viking stood on the shore watching the flames.

Where are the others? There are but thirty men here.

Skald walked all the way up to the group without being seen. Everyone was too intent on watching the flames. He searched the line, but could see no sign of Tor. The Captain was clearly visible in his long wolf's cloak. Skald touched him on the shoulder... and nearly fell on his arse when Tor turned and looked down at him.

Tor clasped him in a bear hug.

"Well met old friend, I thought we had lost you too." Tor said, then stood back when he saw the group of followers behind the Skald.

"I see you have found some friends," Tor said.

Skald smiled.

"And I see you have found a new cloak. And a sword. We have tales to tell each other."

Tor nodded.

"But not now. We need to get to shelter."

For the first time Skald noticed how drawn and tired his friend looked. That, and something else. He looked older and bigger somehow.

He has become Viking.

"Come," Skald said. "We can fit some in the cave, but not those from the other boats."

Tor had a lost, forlorn look.

"There are no others Skald. We are all that have come out of the water."

Skald didn't get time to reply, nor even to digest the information, as Kai turned and saw him, then looked past him.

He laughed bitterly.

"First trolls and now fucking dwarfs. Are we yet in Midgard or have we truly come to Swartheim?"

One of his henchmen stepped forward, sword raised, stepping in front of Baren.

"Let us kill them Captain. Kill them and be done

with this place," he said

Skald stepped between the man and the woman. Tor moved to join him.

"We have need of the hospitality of these people if we are to survive this night," Tor said.

"People?" Kai spat out a laugh. "Such as these are not people."

Baden pulled at Skald's cloak.

They are better people than you Kai Persson.

Tor and Kai stared at each other, hands on swords, neither moving

Skald realised that he had missed something important. But now wasn't the time to consider it.

"Come then Tor," Skald said. "You at least shall share their hospitality with me. The rest can take their chances with the *Alma* if that is what they wish."

Still Tor did not move. Then he relaxed, and laughed.

"I believe you have the correct plan Skald," he said. "But we must do as our Captain commands. However I am certain our Captain does not want his charges standing on this beach all night. Is that not right *Captain*?"

Kai eyed Tor suspiciously, then looked away.

Bjorn the sail-master came to stand beside Skald and Tor. Five other Viking moved to join them.

Tor could be Captain. Mayhap he should be.

Then he had no more time to think. Baren pulled at his cloak once more and, with the mummery, explained that the *Alma* would return, as soon as the fire from the boat died down.

Skald nodded.

He looked from Tor to Kai.

"We must go now. The *Alma* have no liking for the fire. But they will return, once the snow and the sea quench the flames."

Indeed the fire on the water seemed to be less bright than before.

Kai seemed unsure. Either that, or he was unwilling to make a decision. A wild roar from out in the storm decided the matter for him.

"We shall shelter with the Skald," he shouted. "In the morning things will be clearer."

Skald led them all back through the settlement, and the fire-wyrm once more snaked up the hill.

15

Tor was last to enter the cave. He had one last look around him before going in, but nothing could be seen in the snow and the wind. There was nothing to show of the battle, no sign that the best man he had ever known beside his own father had gone to Valhalla. He strained, hoping to hear the noise of good cheer and the banging of shields as a newcomer was welcomed into the Halls.

But there was only the mournful whistle of the wind, bringing with it a biting cold, even through the thickness of the wolf-cloak.

He stepped inside the cave, and immediately wished he had stayed outside. A thick, musty smell hung heavy in the air, and with the press of bodies and the burning firebrands it was stiflingly warm. But he hardly had space to lift his arms from his side, never mind remove the fur cloak.

He did a quick headcount of the Viking.

Thirty. Thirty out of near a hundred. By Odin's name, these beasts will pay dearly for that.

Skald pushed his way through the crowd to Tor's side.

"There is something I must show you," Skald said. "Then we will tell our tales."

Tor let himself be led over to a long wall. As he crossed the cave small hands reached for him, stroking the fur of his cloak.

Skald stopped in front of a long frieze that had been carved into the wall.

"This tells the story of these people," he started. Tor listened as the story was laid out for him. Skald was about to show him the silver pendant when Tor spotted Kai watching them.

"Keep it hidden," he said softly. "And do not tell the others."

Tor told the tale of Per's ending, tears flowing down his cheeks as the memory of the immolation came flooding back. When he finished, he sat in silence, neither he, nor Skald, having the words to hide the depth of their despair.

They were not alone. Injured or not, the Viking present all felt the loss of their Captain deeply, though none spoke of it.

The small people did their best to be hospitable, and handed round endless bowls of fish stew, and a fermented brew made of milk that smelled terrible, but proved far more potent than any mead. Coupled with the perils of the day and the shock of losing so many comrades, most of the Viking took to it with gusto. There was none of the merriment that usually accompanied their drinking. No songs were sung, no tales told, and the women of the small people were left alone as Viking after Viking descended into their cups as fast as the cups would allow.

"Skald," Kai called out. "A tale. A tale to lift our mood this night."

"Our mood is as it should be," Tor said.

Kai tried to stand, but fell backward too drunk to maintain balance.

"You will do as your Captain commands," he shouted, still trying to sit up.

Tor moved forward, but Bjorn held him back.

"Best do as the Captain says," the sail-master said. "And do not press the matter. The lad has lost his father."

Aye, Tor thought. *But his mood is not as it should be.*

"It is of no matter," Skald said to Tor as he stood. "I am Skald. This is what I am here for."

Skald started to recite, and the Viking grew quiet.

Long ago there was a fisher-wife who lost her husband. Blaming the Gods, she called down a curse on them, and her curses reached to Asgard itself where the lambs died and the harvest rotted and the sea gave up neither whale nor fish for a year.

Odin saw, and with Loki visited her, and pleaded with her to lift the spell. She replied that she would...if the Gods could raise a laugh in her, for she had not laughed since her husband had died.

So Odin took out his glass eye, and pulled faces, then made the eye appear to look out of his ear, his mouth, and even his belly button. And through it all the fisher-wife remained stony-faced.

Then it was the turn of Loki. Taking off his belt he looped one end around the horns of a goats in the field around the fisher-wife's cottage. The other end he looped around his testicles. Then he roared, scaring the goat so much that it took off at speed, dragging Loki along behind it by his balls.

Loki screamed in pain.

The fisher-wife laughed for a week.

The curse was lifted. The woman had learned to laugh again, Loki had learned something of the ways of the female mind, and Odin had learned how far Loki was prepared to go to get his own way. None of the three would forget the lessons they learned that day.

Several Viking laughed, but their hearts were not in it. Tor smiled ruefully as Kai, stretched out on his back on a fur rug, started to snore, ropy drool dribbling from the corner of his mouth.

"There lies our fine Captain," Bjorn said, arriving at his side.

Tor spat on the ground.

"If we survive this Viking, I shall never follow him," he said.

"Nor shall I lad," Bjorn said. "But come. You too

must rest. We will have much to do on the morrow."

A small fur clad person – Tor was not sure whether it was male or female – showed him to a rocky shelf that was laid out in furs. Skald was already nearby, sleeping, but not soundly. His eyes shifted wildly behind their lids, and he muttered to himself, about *Jotun* and stone.

"Hush Orjan," Tor said, laying a hand on his friend's brow. "You can be Skald again in the morning."

Skald went quiet, and started to snore. Tor smiled and laid himself down on the furs. He was asleep almost before he rested his head.

He woke to sunshine in the cave mouth and the sound of Viking paying dearly for the excesses of the night before. He hadn't thought it possible, but the stench in the cave was worse now than before. Skald was no longer there on the furs nearby, so Tor went outside in the hope of meeting him, and some fresher air.

Kai sat in the cave mouth, head in his hands and groaning.

"Fucking dwarfs," he said as Tor passed. "Cannot even make proper mead." He coughed, spluttered, then had to hang his head over the side of the cliff as a milky white fluid came up.

"Have a good morning *Captain*," Tor said, and was almost cheerful as he made his way down the slope in the morning sunshine. The snow had frozen into a crisp crust that crackled underfoot, and the wind had fallen to the merest whisper. Tor's better mood lasted only as long as it took him to look down at the smoking ruins of the three longboats.

He got to the shore to find Bjorn directing salvage operations.

Skald sat on a rock, staring out to sea, lost in the wyrd. Tor knew there would be no talking to him for quite some time. He walked over to where Bjorn inspected a large piece of sailcloth washed up on the beach.

"Can we save anything?

"Nary a thing," the older man said. "Mayhap about a third of the hull of the *Firewyrm* where the wind kept the worst of the flame off, but that will be about all."

"Provisions?"

Bjorn shook his head.

"We found two braziers, kept intact due to being iron, but everything that could burn has gone. We have a full sail, but no boat to put it on."

Tor motioned around at the forests on the hillside.

"Can we rebuild? We only have need of one boat."

"I have been wondering that myself lad. That decision is for the Captain to make."

Tor stared out at the black scarred skeletons of the longboats.

"Are there any bodies?" he whispered.

Bjorn kept his voice low.

"Nary a one," he said. "Neither Viking nor beast. And there is worse. Come."

He led Tor to the far end of the shore where the sea loch butted close up against the forest. A small patch of snow covered gravel was all that separated the water from the tree line. Footprints studded the snow – deep, wide footprints too large and too heavy to be made by men. Alongside some of the prints were long deep gouges that went down through the snow into the gravel below leaving brown runnels that were easily followed.

Drag marks.

"The bodies have been dragged away?"

Bjorn nodded.

"Then we must follow," Tor said. "We cannot leave them in the hands of those beasts."

"Follow?" Kai said behind them. "Follow who?"

"Our kinsmen," Bjorn said. "The beasts have taken their bodies. Without proper burial, they will never find Valhalla."

Kai looked into the forest then spat in the gravel.

"There will be no following," he said. "See to your boat-building sail-master. I want to be on the water and out of here in three days."

He did not give Bjorn time to reply as he turned and went back along the shore, pausing only to throw up more of the milky-white fluid.

Bjorn looked at the forest, then back at the boats.

"We must obey. He is our Captain."

Tor said nothing, and stood looking into the woods for many minutes after Bjorn had left to continue the salvage.

16

Skald came out of the wyrd with a start, almost falling off the rock on which he sat. He was confused by what it had shown him, for all he had seen was a retelling of *Loki's Testicles* as he'd told it in the cave. It was a comic story that he'd told often in the Great Hall, for it always amused the wife of the Thane, even on the twentieth telling.

Why would the wyrd show me the old story? Why tell me about Loki?

He wasn't given time to think. Most of the Viking were now down on the shore, some helping with the salvage, others merely standing, staring in horror at the ruin the fire had made of the longboats.

"Viking. To me," Kai called out. Everyone responded. Some moved faster than others, and many still looked pale and sick from too much fermented brew. Soon the surviving Viking had all gathered around.

"We will not cower in the cave with the dwarfs another night," Kai said. "I need five men to work with Bjorn on the boat. The rest will build. I want a stockade around the central huts. And I want it done before nightfall."

At first the Viking did not move, but Kai's three henchmen stood beside him, and one by one the men moved off to start work.

Tor stood, unmoving, staring at Kai.

Kai broke first, turning on his heels.

Bjorn dragged Tor and Skald away.

"Come lads. Let us build our Captain his boat."

And so began one of the weariest days of Skald's life. They spent the morning dragging timbers out of the freezing water and sorting them on the shore, burnt from merely singed. The shore and area around them soon became a slushy mess, so cold that Skald ceased to feel his toes after only ten minutes, and after an hour he was sure that his feet were no more flesh, but had instead turned completely to ice. By the time they broke for rest Skald's whole left leg felt like a cold slab of stone, and it moved about as easily.

"We can do this Orjan," Tor said, coming to sit beside him. "You should rest. I have not seen you so pale since the night of the fall."

"Please do not remind me," Skald said. "At least then I was lying swathed in hot furs with a fire to warm me."

"Rest then," Tor said. "No one will think less of you."

Yes, they will.

Tor was blind when it came to how others saw him, but Skald did not have that luxury. He knew he was seen as *weak.* He would never be Viking, and the men all knew that. They thought him feeble, and they were afraid of the wyrd. In combination, that was enough for them to already think less of him. If he did not work with the rest of them, it would be just another step lower for his status among them, and he was already near as low as he could get.

"Just give me five minutes," Skald said. "The leg will ease. I will work."

Tor looked like he might say something, but he kept quiet.

Skald was thankful that his friend didn't press the matter.

For, in truth, I might weaken and do as he says.

And I would only regret it later.

The small people brought a hot fish stew. It contained too much salt, and only warmed a small part of his insides, but the rest had given time for some feeling to creep back into his leg.

Then it was time to get to work hewing timber from the forest. Twenty Viking worked among the trees, and every one of them looked at least once to the high ground above them. No man was ever more than six feet from a weapon or ten feet from a fellow Viking.

But the *Alma* did not come.

I almost wish they would, if it means I can rest.

He was immediately disgusted by the thought. But all afternoon he had watched as the stockade was built and stakes were laid. The structure had taken shape, and already they were at work building an interior walkway.

They are making better progress than we are on the boat at least.

The sail master announced they had cut enough timber. It was all laid out along the beach, a mixture of old and new timbers of varying lengths. Now Bjorn had them sorting it into piles. Skald shifted wood until his hands bled and his leg could hardly take his weight. And still he worked, only his will keeping him going. The men grumbled and complained against the cold and damp, but Skald said nothing, lost in a world where all he knew was how to lift a piece of wood and place it somewhere else.

The sun was going down when Bjorn finally called a halt for the day. Skald sat back on the same rock as before and was not sure he would ever be able to stand again. Every muscle in his body cried out for rest, and he could scarcely remember anything of the day beyond the pain. Viking began to head for the shelter of the stockade, where smoke told of fire, heat and sustenance, but Skald could not stand, could not get his arse up from the cold rock.

It was Baren who got him moving. She arrived in a

hurry, and did her mummer's play of the *Alma* that Skald was starting to know only too well.

It was so comical that he laughed, and forgot how tired he was. It obvious that she did not find it funny. She danced around him, clearly agitated, gaze flickering between Skald and the gathering shadows under the trees.

Finally he caught her meaning.

"Tor," Skald called. "They are coming."

Baren grabbed Skald's arm and heaved him to his feet, so fast that he nearly tumbled over. Only his staff saved him from going headfirst to the ground. She kept pulling, insistent, dragging him along the shore. She pointed up the hill to their hiding place, and pulled hard at him again.

"Tor," he called. "She asks for us to go to the cave."

Tor strode over and stood beside them.

"Kai will not go," he said. "He mistrusts these people."

"Kai is an idiot."

"Hush," Tor said. "We all know it. But he is Captain. We must do his will, or forfeit our own lives."

"Do his will? Even he himself does not know what that is."

"Nevertheless, that is what must be."

"This cannot be right."

"Mayhap not," Tor said. "But it is our way. We follow him until he is dead, then we choose another."

"Then maybe *someone* should make sure he dies soon," Skald whispered. "For the good of those that remain."

Tor looked shocked, as if a great sacrilege had been committed.

"If another had said that, I might have killed him on the spot," he replied. "Do not ask me of this again Skald. I will not go against the Viking way."

Skald turned his back and took the old woman's hand.

"If you will not go, then I will," he said. "If Kai wants a Skald, tell him to come to the cave. I will have no more of this foolishness."

He waited just long enough to see if Tor would follow.

He did not.

"You will die on this beach," Skald called back.

"Then I die as Viking," Tor replied.

The last Skald saw of his friend was the wolf's cloak swinging as he walked into the new stockade alongside sail-master Bjorn.

17

The stockade gate was sealed behind them as soon as the last man came in from the shore.

"Where is the Skald?" Bjorn asked.

"With the small people," Tor replied. "He wishes to learn more about them."

"They are short, they are ugly and they smell," Bjorn said laughing. "What else is there to know?"

That is what I am wondering.

He was remembering the carving on the cave wall, and the silver pendant they had given to Skald. Obviously there was more to be learned. But Tor knew well enough that only Skald would have the wits to do the learning. He looked up the hill to where Skald slowly followed the small woman up the path. Even from here Tor could see that his friend's limp was much worse than it had been earlier.

He will be safe. And my place is here. Where there is fighting to be done.

He put all thought of Skald to the back of his mind, content to know that his friend was in a place that had obviously kept the small people from harm for many generations. He remembered Per's last words to him.

Someone will have to keep the men together. Kai does not have it in him. Keep them together, and bring them safe home to Ormsdale. For me?

He turned his attention to the defences. Kai had ordered them built, but good Viking strength had done the real work, and Tor noted with satisfaction that they had built well. The stockade was built of newly hewn timber, a thick sap still fresh and running down the sides in places. It stood nearly ten feet high, two logs thick all the way round, and looked to be thirty yards across at its widest, encompassing the *eyes, nose and mouth* huts of the face he'd seen earlier from above. The outer circle of huts lay beyond a ring of tall pointed stakes facing out from the base of the stockade wall at a sharp angle, each no more than two feet from the next. Firebrands had been placed at six-foot intervals along an internal walkway, which was patrolled by Viking carrying tall spears.

"They have done better than I had expected," Tor said to Bjorn.

There was a harsh laugh behind them, and they turned to see Kai and his henchmen.

"Mayhap your *Captain* is right after all?" Kai said. "A good Viking wall is more fitting protection than a dwarf's cave."

"Mayhap we shall find out what our *Captain* is made of when the beasts return," Tor said. "Will you be leading the defence, or hiding in the midden like a maiden?"

Kai's eyes flared in anger.

"When we return to Ormsdale, I will stand before the Thane in the Great Hall, and you will return that sword, and that cloak, to its rightful owner."

Tor laughed at him.

"And I shall continue to wear it in honour of its *rightful* owner until that day comes."

Two of the henchmen reached for their swords, but Bjorn stepped forward.

He looked Kai in the eye.

"A good Captain knows whom his best men are when a fight is coming," he said.

Kai took his eyes from Tor and looked at Bjorn.

"There is a fight coming," he said. "I will grant you that much."

Once more he turned away to avoid Tor's stare. His henchmen followed.

Tor spat at the ground.

"You should have let him try," he said to Bjorn.

The sail-master shook his head.

"We will need every man before this night is out. I can feel it. Besides," he said, clapping Tor on the shoulder. "There will be another time. He will not always walk away."

"Good," Tor replied. "For I am ready for him."

Night came quickly, a star-studded night with a full moon that reminded Tor all too much of the white faces of the *Alma*.

"Come inside lad," Bjorn said. "It will be colder than a witches teat's tonight, and you'll need some stew inside you."

Tor shook his head.

"I shall stay," he said.

Someone should.

Kai had gone into the largest roundhouse near on an hour ago, and had not shown his face again since. After twenty minutes Tor had taken it on himself to walk the stockade, talking to the guards, showing them that someone cared that they were out in the cold keeping watch. Two of the guards had called him *Captain*.

He did not correct them.

He walked the circumference of the walkway, finishing above the gate. Snow gleamed, silver in the moonlight, light dancing off the trees like faerie spirits.

Overhead *Odin's Wagon* straddled the sky.

Look down on us tonight Odin. Look down, and send us your protection. For we shall have need of it.

He dropped his gaze from the sky, checking the stockade, then the rest of the huts of the outer circle. Finally, he looked high up on the hill. A red glow showed at the cave mouth where the small people had retreated to safety.

Be well Skald.

Part of Tor would have been happy, up there in the cave, drinking some fermented milk and listening to Skald recite the old tales. But the other part, the larger part, could scent a battle coming. His blood sang and his arm forever reached for the hilt of the sword at his side. The beasts had killed the nearest thing he had to a father.

And they will pay dearly for it.

Bjorn came and joined him on the wall.

"Jarryd has found some barrels of fish oil in the huts. It is foul stuff, but it will burn well enough. Come, help me get them up on the parapet. We will have need of them I think."

For the next ten minutes Tor helped to heft the barrels of oil, ten of them. They placed them at intervals around the walkway, each near a firebrand. As they placed the last barrel down, Tor thought he caught a flash of white from between the trees at the shoreline, but when he turned there was only deep shadow.

Tor and Bjorn walked the perimeter, checking the defences.

"We have done as much as we can lad," Bjorn said, "*Now* will you take some food?"

At the thought, Tor's stomach rumbled loudly, like distant thunder. He followed Bjorn into the roundhouse and accepted a bowl of stew that was thrust at him. Kai sat silently at the hearth alongside his three henchmen. Tor and Bjorn ate in silence, but Tor could see that most of the men were tense, expecting an attack at any moment.

If Skald were here, he would tell a tale, remind them of glory. Remind them that they are Viking.

Tor stood.

"We have no mead or ale," he said. "But I would

have a toast, even if it is only with this stew."

He raised his bowl.

"Last night we lost many Viking. We lost our Captain."

His voice grew stronger as he warmed to the task.

"They are out there, the beasts that killed our brothers. When they come, we will show them the error they have made. We will send them to Helheim where they belong."

He raised his bowl again.

"To our dead. We shall avenge them."

Many of the Viking stood and hailed him. All save Kai and his henchmen. They sat at the hearth, brows like thunder, saying nothing.

Tor finished the stew and headed back out to the wall, expecting an attack at any moment. But none came, and when Tor's turn for patrol arrived, the man he replaced told him to expect nothing but a cold boring watch.

"The fire has scared them away," the man said. "We shall not see them again."

Tor thought otherwise. He had seen the beasts closer than most.

They will come. They are too much like us not to.

But for several hours it went as the man said. Tor's head ached from the strain of peering into the dark shadows under the trees, and he had to walk briskly along the parapet to stop the chill settling in his bones. High on the hill the red glow from the cave showed bright in the darkness. Waves lapped on the shore, bringing the soft rattle of pebbles as they receded. But there was no sign of the *Alma*.

Halfway through his watch Bjorn brought him another bowl of fish stew.

"Drink it fast lad," the sail master said. "It tastes even fouler now than it did earlier, but it is warm, and that is the important thing."

Bjorn looked out over the beach as Tor ate.

"Kai talked to me," he said in a whisper. "He wanted to know how quickly I could have a boat, any boat, ready. He is still sitting by the hearth in the hut, shivering like a maiden on her wedding night, shitting in his boots at the thought of another fight."

He spat over the parapet.

"How Per managed to father one such as that I shall never know. I have talked with the others," he said. "We will follow you if you wish it."

I wish it. But I cannot.

"For better or worse," Tor said. "He is Per's son, and Captain by right. I cannot kill him."

Bjorn spoke softly.

"And if someone else were to do the job for you? What then?"

Tor was spared having to answer as the first noise came in the silent night.

There was a soft *whuff*, then a high pitched hooting that echoed around the hills.

At first Tor took it for an owl, for it did indeed sound similar to the hunting calls of the snow-white owls that arrived around Ormsdale in the first days of winter. But these calls were deeper, and where the owls hunted in pairs, this call was answered by many more, dozens more, out in the forest to the east of the settlement.

The night air was full of the sound, which rose, and rose again into a wailing howl. Tor had heard something like it once before, when a wolf pack was choosing a leader, but that had not shaken him all the way down to the bones like this did. The wail caused his helm to vibrate and thrum against his ears, and loosened his bowels such that he thought he might shit right there and then.

"Rouse the men," Tor said. "They are here."

Even as Bjorn left his side, the first of the *Alma* walked out of the trees.

It was a big male, silvery-white in the moonlight, almost glowing. It stood there for ten seconds, looking around the settlement, and studying the stockade. Tor lifted a spear from where it leaned on the wall, but the distance was too far to contemplate.

He watched the beast, and it watched him. If this one had been in the fight the night before it showed no sign of it. There were no wounds on its body, and it rippled with muscle under sleek fur. It was difficult to gauge its size, but it could not be less than nine feet tall. The head was even more conical at the rear than any Tor had seen before, and even from the front the shaggy mane showed, being blown in a slight breeze.

It put huge hands to its mouth, pursed its lips, and *hooted,* five times in quick succession.

As if from nowhere, a horde of tall white figures strode out from the shadows.

They were all large males, and Tor lost count at forty. They stood behind the first one on the shore.

He is the leader. They wait for his commands.

Once more Tor considered the spear. If he could take out their leader this battle might be over before it had begun. He gauged the distance.

No matter how many times I look, it will still be too far.

Behind him he heard the sounds of Viking preparing for battle. The shadows in the stockade flickered in black and red as all the firebrands were lit and the air was suddenly full of the stench of oily smoke.

The *Alma* began to shuffle forward slowly.

I hope we have built this stockade as well as it looks. For we will need it this night.

In seconds all of the Viking were armed and arranged around the walkway. But the beasts showed no signs of being in a hurry. The big male strode, in long loping strides, along the beach, inspecting the timbers that had been laid along its length. It picked up a log that had taken three men to carry and threw it aside casually, sending it rattling across the stony shore. It sniffed at the burnt pieces from the longboats, and raked through them with his feet. Finding nothing, it *hooted* again, and Tor thought there might have been a tone of derision in the sound.

The beast walked back along the shore to the settlement and inspected the empty huts in the outer circle, walking completely around one of them, pulling at the thatched roof, pounding a huge hand against the stone wall. It came to the midden where the Viking had killed the first female and stood, head bowed, for long seconds.

It is mourning their dead.

There is where we made our mistake. Odin save us, and allow us time yet to make some more.

Bjorn once more came to Tor's side.

"Mayhap they are merely curious?"

Tor laughed bitterly.

"I think we both know better than that by now friend. They are beasts made for fighting. And we have brought their blood to a boil. Mayhap if we had let the female leave, then we may have avoided this. But now the fight is coming. And we brought it on ourselves."

The big male bent to the shore and hefted a rock bigger than a man's head with as little effort as Tor would have made if lifting a pebble. Without warning it threw the stone, straight at the stockade. Tor flinched and ducked involuntarily, but the rock was missing them by some way. It hit the wall five yards to his right. A large chunk of wood split away and the whole wall rang with the shock.

The beast hooted loudly, and the *Alma* behind him came forward.

"Do we have any archers?" Tor asked.

Bjorn shook his head.

"We recovered but one bow from the longboats, and no arrows."

Tor looked out to where the beasts stood. They bent, and started to lift rocks from the shore.

"Then pray to Odin that this wall is as strong at it looks," Tor said. "For it is about to be tested."

There was a dull thud as a rock hit the wall only feet from them.

"And it might be best to keep our heads down," Tor said as they ducked under the level of the timbers.

Rocks struck all along the wall, rattling like heavy hail on a helm. Splinters of wood flew in the air. Some rocks flew over the wall to crash heavily onto the ground. One particularly large stone crashed clear through the roof of one of the huts inside the stockade. Tar Petrsson lifted his head too high above the parapet and a rock caught him full in the face, crushing his skull like an eggshell. A larger rock hit the gate and the wood *cracked*, like a sudden thunderclap from an overhead storm.

"Will the wall hold?" Bjorn shouted.

Tor chanced a look around the stockade. The attack was concentrated on an area near them, just to the right of the main gate.

"If they target the gate we will surely be in trouble," he said. "But the wood here is strong. It will splinter and bend. But it will not break. Not unless they start throwing larger rocks."

"Then let us pray they are not as strong as they look," Bjorn said.

Rocks continued to rain down on the stockade, and

no man would lift his head above the parapet for fear of losing it.

18

Skald was asleep and dreaming. He knew it was a dream; he remembered falling into it, and could *feel* his sleeping body as a presence some way removed from him. His leg still hurt, and that also told him this was a dream, for in the wyrd, his body was always whole again and pain free.

Where the wyrd and Midgard felt like two aspects of the same reality, the place where he was now was far removed from either. He floated in a vast empty blackness, with no sense of either up or down. He hung there for a long time, but felt no urgency to move -- no panic. He merely waited, curious to see what would happen next.

"For sure, this is the strangest dream ever. At least the fever dreams after the fall had something happening in them, even if they made no sense."

But eventually he became aware of movement, far away at first, but getting closer all the while.

Something danced in the dark, something huge and heavy. He felt it first through the soles of his feet, but soon his whole frame shook, vibrating in time with the rhythm. His head swam, and it seemed as if the very darkness melted and ran. He was alone, in a vast cathedral of emptiness where nothing existed save the dark and the pounding beat from below.

Shapes began to move in the dark; wispy shadows with no substance, shadows that capered and whirled as the dance grew ever more frenetic.

He was buffeted, as if by a strong, surging tide, but as the beat grew ever stronger he cared little. He gave himself to it, lost in the dance, lost in the dark.

Voices rose in a chant, but he understood none of it.

It did not matter. He was at peace. He floated up and away from the other dancers, away from the darkness, ending high above where he was finally able to look down.

A vast figure lay bound on a huge high plinth. From this distance Skald could not make out any details. But he could clearly see the Alma.

All around the bound giant, the hairy ones danced.
Scores of them.

He woke, confused. It was if the dance went on, for he still heard a rhythm. But there was no dance to this, or if there was it was a frenzied jig that he wanted no part of.

The noise came from outside the cave. He made his way to the mouth. Three of the small people blocked his way, insistent that he should stay inside.

The noise sounded louder still here, and it was driving Skald to distraction that he did not know its source. He pushed at the small people, but they would not budge. He pushed harder, angry now. Still they did not move.

He screamed in rage, and they jumped, almost as if he'd hit them. Their eyes went wide and they cowered away from him, moving quickly out of his way.

Skald suddenly felt ashamed at scaring them.

But I do not have time for apologies.

He went out onto the ledge. When he looked down on the settlement below it felt like his heart stopped and he had to force himself to breathe.

The moon lit the whole scene in sharp outline. The *Alma* stood in a group on the shore where it butted up to the edge of the forest, throwing rock after rock at the stockade.

The stones flew in high arcs, tumbling through the air. Skald felt a heavy pain in his leg and the memory of his own tumble down the scree slope came vividly to mind. But even when he had finally stopped rolling and hit bottom that fateful day, it had not been with the force with which these missiles hit the stockade.

If it had been, I would be in much smaller pieces.

Even from high above the noise was almost deafening. Chunks of wood flew in the air from the stockade wall, and Viking cowered on the walkway, unable to lift their heads.

The wall will hold.

He could see that, and had just relaxed a fraction when a large male *Alma* raised hands to his lips and *hooted.*

The barrage of rocks stopped.

The big male strode forward and inspected the stockade wall from a distance. Skald couldn't see its face, but imagined an air of puzzlement being there. Small piles of rock lay at the base of the stockade wall. The wood was pocked with scars that showed as white streaks in the moonlight. In two places the outermost of the timbers had broken and fallen off leaving a jagged stump.

But the wall held.

The beast strode all the way round the stockade.

He is looking for weaknesses.

When it returned to the shore the beast raised its hands to its lips and *hooted* loudly.

A group of *Alma* advanced on the stockade.

The siege proper had begun.

19

It finally fell quiet.

The Viking stayed under the parapet, fearing a possible trap.

All was still for almost a minute.

"Is it over?" Bjorn said, whispering.

"There is only one way to know," Tor said.

He risked a look over the battlement. The beasts were all still there, lined up along the shore. The large male lifted his hands to his lips and *hooted. Alma* advanced on the stockade, silently, like white ghosts, steam rising off them in the chill night, giving them an almost spectral air.

"It is not over. It is only just beginning," Tor said.

All around the stockade Viking still knelt or sat below the level of the wall where they had cowered during the barrage.

Where is Kai? He should be rallying them.

There was no time to wait.

"To arms," Tor called loudly. "Make ready. They are coming."

All along the wall Viking stood and stared at the beasts.

"In the name of Odin," a man standing near Tor said. "We cannot fight such as these. We must flee."

Bjorn smacked the speaker hard across the face with a gloved hand, rocking his head sideways and bringing a gout of blood from his nose.

"We stand. If we die, then it is the will of the Gods, and we will tell tales of it in Valhalla," Bjorn said.

The man looked at him sullenly.

Bjorn drew his sword.

"You have a choice," he said, showing the bloodied man the blade. "Fight like a man, or die like a dog."

The man backed away, wiping blood from his nose. But there was no more talk of fleeing.

Bjorn raised his sword and shouted.

"We are Viking!"

"We are Viking," the men responded, and beat a rhythm against the wall of the stockade with sword and spear. They started a chant, well known to Tor from many nights in the Great Hall. He had never expected to be singing it to beasts such as these. Every man joined in and the pounding song echoed in the hills even as it stirred Tor's blood, readying it for battle.

Hail, Viking! Hail, sons of Viking!
Now is the time for glory and blood
Now is the time for strength and iron
Our fathers in Valhalla await us.
We shall meet in the halls of the brave.

Hearing the noise the *Alma* raised their heads and as one gave out a series of barking coughs as they came on, a martial rhythm in time with their steps.

A battle song. They too have songs.

Tor realised they had seriously underestimated the intelligence of their enemy, but it became a moot point very quickly as the *Alma* walked to the foot of the wall and started to methodically break up the stakes that had been placed there. They threw huge logs aside as if they were mere twigs, and tore at the wall itself.

The Viking had been expecting a group of uncoordinated beasts that would attack them blindly, giving them the chance to pick them off one at a time.

And now we shall be undone by our hubris.

Splinters flew as the beast's talons tore at the wood. The heads of the creatures were several feet below Tor, but he would have had to lean over too far to get in a killing blow, and he was reluctant to get anywhere close to the reach of one of those huge hands.

"Oil," Tor called. "Use the oil. It is all that will save us."

Below Tor two of the beasts had already torn all the stakes away and loosened one of the timbers of the main wall. Bjorn heaved a barrel up onto the lip and Tor removed the bung, gagging at the acrid stench that arose from the oil.

The sail-master poured more than half of the thick foul liquid down the side of the wall where it formed a slick. It pooled at the beasts' feet and confused them enough that they stopped their attack on the defences to investigate. One of them bent and rubbed a huge palm in the fluid. It lifted the hand to its mouth and its nostrils flared in disgust at the stench, making it draw the hand away quickly. More slowly now, it licked the palm with a massive red meaty tongue, drew back its lips and looked up at Tor.

Not only do they have songs. They also smile.
But they will not smile for long.

The beasts returned to their assault on the wall.

"They are almost through," Bjorn shouted.

Tor dropped a firebrand, just as the beasts tore a large timber free. They tried to force their bodies through a small gap into the stockade, and roared with rage when they found the gap too narrow.

The firebrand hit the ground and lit the oil. It went up with a *whoosh,* the heat of it singeing Tor's eyebrows as he pulled back. He just had time to watch the fire catch in the fur of the *Alma* before the flame spread up the wall and he had to retreat away from the heat.

Below him the squeals and screams of beasts were terrible to hear. All along the wall the same act was being played out. The air filled with the stench of burning hair and flesh and a dense black smoke hung like a pall over the wall.

Now it was Tor's turn to smile, although there was little humour in it.

The smell of cooking flesh started him salivating and he gagged, almost threw up, at the thought. He had eaten bear meat on a hunt last winter, but somehow that was different. These beasts, whatever they were, were close enough to men to make the thought of eating them a sickening one, and he felt ill to the pit of his stomach.

Screams finally, thankfully, fell away to piteous moans.

Then, finally, the night fell quiet except for the crack and crackle where the walls of the stockade yet burned.

He looked out over the settlement. The large male stood, watching as *Alma* burned. A dozen of them lay charred and still at the base of the stockade.

The beast showed no concern for the dead. Instead it watched the flames intently.

And soon, so did Tor, for parts of the stockade were now well aflame. The patch of wall where Bjorn had poured the oil burned furiously, as if the oil itself had sunk into the wood turning it into a huge firebrand. The wood cracked and spat, sending smoking sparks flying high into the air.

Bjorn stood at Tor's side.

"At least we shall not perish from the cold," the sail-master said.

They both watched the fires.

"Shall we put out the flames?" Tor asked.

"We are caught between the rocks and the maelstrom," Bjorn said. "If we put out the flame, the beasts will attack and overrun us. If we do not, the stockade will burn and *then* the beasts will attack."

Out on the shore the remaining *Alma* showed no

sign of being in a hurry.

"Mayhap we can choose a third way," Tor said. "Do we have any oil remaining?"

"I have half a barrel here," Bjorn said. "And there will be more. By my count there are six fires burning. If luck is with us we may yet have three or four barrels worth."

Tor smiled grimly.

"It will have to be enough."

"What are you thinking lad?"

Tor was thinking of Per, walking among the Alma on the longboat, touching them with flame. But now was not the time to remind the sail-master of the death of their Captain.

"Mayhap we can trap them and lure them in," he said. "Let us discover just how much like us these beasts are."

It took ten minutes for Tor to prepare his plan. In that time the walls burned further, but there were no breaches, and the *Alma* stayed back on the shore, well away from the flames.

Kai arrived just as they were finishing preparations. He looked flushed, but it wasn't exertion or excitement that Tor saw there. He realised with disgust that it was fear.

Tor spat at Kai's feet.

"Where were you when the beast's attacked? Shitting your breeks again?"

"You cannot speak to me like that. I am your Captain."

Tor laughed in his face.

"Then mayhap you need to start acting like a Captain. A Captain would have been on the wall with his men, not cowering inside like a maid."

Kai's hand went to his sword, but Tor didn't flinch.

He just smiled again.

Kai looked to Bjorn for help.

"We must flee," he said. "We must go back to the cave. We will be safe there."

Bjorn and Tor both laughed.

"Safe? You wish safety?" Tor said, disbelieving. "What kind of *Viking* are you?"

"There's the gate," Bjorn said to Kai, pointing. "Do not let it bang you on the arse on the way out."

Kai was getting desperate, his voice high and whining.

"If we leave now, we can take the firebrands. The beasts will not attack us. They fear the flame."

Again Tor laughed.

"I doubt these *beasts* fear much of anything at all. But go, if you must. Take as many with you as will follow. We Viking will stand."

Kai looked around the men. His three *lapdogs* walked to his side, but no one else moved.

"I am your Captain," he called. "You *must* follow me."

"We are Viking," Bjorn said quietly. "And we stand."

"Defy me, and your lives will be forfeit when we return to Ormsdale," Kai shouted. Tor saw that the man was close to tears.

His father would be ashamed to see him like this.

"Then they are forfeit," Tor said quietly. "It shall be better to die bravely here than to run home with our heads hanging low and be branded cowards."

"I *order* you to follow me."

No one moved to join him.

"Fools," he said, and spat at Tor's feet. He lifted a firebrand and headed for the gate. He put a hand on the locking timber just as a deep pounding started on the other side of it. The timbers shook, and more sparks flew from the nearest fire, but the gate held.

For now.

Kai backed away fast.

"It seems you must stand with the rest of us," Tor said, smiling. "Try not to disgrace the memory of your father."

Even as Tor spoke a white arm appeared at the top of the wall above the gate, grasping for grip. The nearest Viking slashed down with his sword and the beast fell away, but, as Tor suspected, they learned fast. Along that stretch of the wall, more hands grasped for purchase, and the defenders were stretched to keep the *Alma* at bay.

"Well lad," Bjorn said. "It seems we have need of a Captain willing to fight. Are you ready for the job?"

"At least as long as this battle lasts," Tor replied. "But that may not be overly long."

He felt a sudden grip of fear and pushed it away angrily.

"Get six more of the men up on the wall. The others I shall need down here."

Tor got the Viking working on his plan while Kai watched on sullenly.

Behind the gate they concentrated the Viking, two ranks of them in a half-circle around a patch of ground on which they piled the roofing materials of the huts. The men stood back while Bjorn and Tor doused the whole area thoroughly with oil.

Tor stood and watched as the thatch sucked up the liquid.

"Will it be sufficient?" Bjorn asked. "We have one barrel remaining."

"It will have to be. I may have use for the remaining one. Open the gate," Tor shouted, and men to either side drew away the timbers that held it closed.

"This ruse will never work," Kai called out. "Listen

to me. We must flee. Mayhap we can reach the forest in safety."

This time most of the men responded by laughing, and Tor smiled grimly.

"If it does not work, we shall be drinking ale in Valhalla within the hour. And we shall explain to your father why you did not happen to be travelling with us."

Then there was no more time for talk. The gate started to swing open under the weight of the doors, only six inches at first.

A hairy arm came through the gap and grabbed at the edge of the door, pushing it open with force. The door swung wildly, hit the inside wall of the stockade with a crash, and fell aside.

A large group of *Alma* cautiously moved inside the stockade.

20

Skald saw the door being thrown open and the *Alma* start to funnel inside, slowly at first, then with more confidence as they were not challenged.

He understood Tor's plan, and had watched his friend organise it with pride.

I am not so sure as he that it will work.

There were now more than ten *Alma* inside the stockade, hemmed into a tight group by spear-carrying Viking. They loomed over the men, the smallest of them head and shoulders taller than even the tallest Viking. Outside the stockade the big male stayed well back on the shore, watching proceedings intently, and a group of nearly twenty more stayed on the beach around him.

They need more of them to enter. Even if the ruse works, they will not kill enough of them.

Inside the stockade the *Alma* advanced toward the Viking. Several of the men stepped back, the tips of their spears shaking and showing their fear.

"Stand firm," Tor called, his voice carrying all the way up to where Skald stood.

"We hold them here."

The Viking put their feet on their spears and created two rows of iron points ahead of the beasts.

Tor stood just behind the two lines, watching the beasts come forward. He hefted a spear and sent it straight into the heart of the nearest Alma, punching through its chest in a spray of blood that covered the beasts behind it.

"Now," Tor shouted, and Skald saw Bjorn light the straw even as the noise of the shout reached him.

The straw burst into a high yellow flame and Skald had to look away from its brightness. The *Alma* howled as they burned, first their legs, then their torsos, the flame getting higher and brighter as it reached the hairy manes down their backs and flared in raging haloes around their heads. The pain sent the beasts into frenzy. They threw themselves at the defending lines.

The Viking had to take a step backward as the weight of two *Alma* hit the spears, but as one the men shoved forward, spears taking the beasts in the chest and forcing them back into their brethren, spreading the flames even further.

One large beast, almost fully aflame, threw itself forward in a leap, trying to jump beyond the iron points of the spears. Tor bent and thrust upwards with the sword, using the *Alma*'s own momentum to let the sword slice from its chest to its groin. Ropy entrails hissed and burned even as they sprayed the defenders with spatters of hot blood.

The *Alma* crashed against a roundhouse wall. Even now it was not yet dead. Its guts hung in a pile on the snow beneath it and flame ran over the length of its body. Yet still it raged. It tried to push itself to its feet and opened its mouth to roar, but only smoke and flame came out of the mouth, and even before Tor could deal a killing blow it finally fell, dead on its face.

The other *Alma* were now a burning mass of fury and rage, throwing themselves every which way in wild attempts to escape the growing flames. The Viking stood firm and their spears did terrible damage to the flaming bodies, thrusting forward again and again, forcing the beasts to chose between the flame and the iron spears.

Most tried to attack the Viking, and when four attempted to escape at the same time the men had to take a step back; heat forcing them to retreat ahead of the beasts. From on high Skald could see that if they retreated any further the line would be weakened irrevocably, and the *Alma* would be able to break free from the cordon.

But Tor had planned for that eventuality.

Tor lifted a barrel and threw it into the melee, raising a plume of thick smoke and fresh sparks from the straw. Flame lapped around the barrel.

The Viking had to take another step back as *Alma* pushed, taking spears into their bodies but ignoring that pain as they tried to escape the greater torture of the fire.

Tor was too late. They will get free.

The oil exploded with a soft *whump* and five *Alma* fell in the blast of heat and flame. Even up on the cliff high above Skald felt the waft of hot air on his face.

Given some respite from the relentless attack the defenders were able to press forward again. Viking spears did their job and quickly dispatched the remaining beasts that were now little more than squirming blackened flesh.

Soon only one *Alma* remained standing, smoking and charred. The flames had eaten at it so much that all its fur was burned away. Its eyes had boiled from their sockets, leaving only black smoking holes. It waved charred ruins of what had once been hands in the air, swatting at flames that had long since been snuffed out. It mewled, a naked piteous thing that wailed like a teething child.

Kill it, Skald whispered. *For pity's sake, kill it.*

Tor sent it to its death with one swift sword stroke to the heart. He stood among the bodies of the fallen *Alma*, flames burning all around him, and stared straight at the large male out on the shore.

With one stroke he took off the *Alma's* head. Sword in one hand and the smoking head in the other, he raised his arms above his head and roared his defiance.

Out on the shore the big *Alma* watched, impassive as Tor drew back his arm and threw the head out of the stockade. It bounced and rolled before stopping, face up, black, smoking eye sockets facing almost straight at Skald. The lips had been burnt off and moonlight showed a yellow-white grin amid the burnt ruin of the head

The big male looked at it, then back at Tor. It *whoofed* twice, then turned, and walked into the forest. The rest of the *Alma* followed silently.

Within seconds the shore was empty, the only sound the crack and spatter of burning wood.

The Viking cheered. They surrounded Tor, clapping him on the back. Skald was the only one to see Kai and his henchmen standing quiet and sullen in the background. A chant went up, echoing around the stockade.

Tor, Tor, Tor.

Skald made to leave the cave and head down to join the others.

Baren held him back, forcibly, shook a finger in his face, then pointed at the forest.

Her meaning was plain.

It is not over.

21

Tor allowed himself a moment to bask in the congratulations of the men. He watched the last of the *Alma* fade like ghosts into the dark forest, and stood for long seconds to make sure a surprise attack was not going to be forthcoming.

We have won.

The men around him seemed sure of it, and indeed, the bragging about their exploits had already begun. By the time they returned to the Great Hall in Ormsdale the beasts would be twelve feet tall, with two heads and breathing fire.

He smiled. He could not begrudge them their moment of victory. But in his heart he knew that was all it would be -- a moment. Finally defeating these beasts would not be that easy. The big male had not looked like a creature that was beaten, and for Tor to assume otherwise would be a grievous mistake. He allowed the men a further minute of backslapping then brought them back to reality.

"Close the gates," Tor shouted. "And douse those fires. We cannot have the walls weakened any further. We may still need their strength this night."

The men moved to comply, all save Kai and his henchmen, who stood to one side, watching Tor's every move.

I shall need to be careful of those, he thought. *For I may get a knife in my back even while watching out for teeth in my throat.*

Once the fires were doused, and even while the wall still steamed, Bjorn came down from the walkway and strode back to Tor's side.

"There is no sign of the beasts on the shore. Have we routed them do you think?"

Tor shook his head.

"We have merely bought ourselves some time. They will be back. And they will have a new strategy. We had best make ready."

Kai stepped forward.

"And how do we do that? You have used up all the oil. Such a trick cannot be done again. The next attack will surely be the end of us. We should all leave now and make for the safety of the cave. Now that they are gone, we have a chance."

Once more Tor shook his head.

"That big one has cunning. He will still be there, just inside the trees. Even now he is watching us, looking for a weakness."

"You cannot know that," Kai said. "I demand that we send someone out to try."

Tor spat at his feet.

"I will not send out any man I can spare," he said. "But *you* can try, any time you like."

"I am Captain here," Kai said, but the petulant whine was back.

Tor turned his back on the man, knowing full well that he was safe for now. He'd heard it in the whine of Kai's voice. The man was afraid, afraid to stand and be Viking -- afraid of Tor.

I will waste no more time on him.

He spoke to Bjorn.

"Get the men back up on the wall," he said. "The beasts will return. And this time, I suspect they will try to surprise us."

Kai laughed.

"They are mere beasts. They cannot *surprise* us."

Tor turned back to him and smiled grimly.

"They have already shown they have more guile than you," he said. "And they are fighting beasts. They will not walk away."

Kai looked like he was about to reply, but he would not look Tor in the eye. He lowered his head and walked away. His henchmen followed.

Tor shouted after them.

"Do not go far Kai," he said. "I shall have need of you."

Bjorn took Tor by the arm.

"Your father would have been proud of you lad," he said. "Without you we might all be dead already."

Tor laughed bitterly.

"Do not thank me too much old man," he said. "The night is not yet over."

For the next hour all was quiet, and Tor began to wonder if he had been wrong about the beasts. But when the attack came, it was sudden, and as surprising as he expected it might be.

Three large *Alma* came out of the forest at a run, moving straight for the gate in a lope, coming fast despite the snow on the ground. Tor sent a spear through the chest of the lead one, but his aim was slightly off and instead of cleaving the heart the spear tore into the muscle at the *Alma*'s shoulder. The beast pulled the weapon out with no more than a flick of its hand and barely slowed, hitting the door full on. The whole stockade shook, then again as the other two arrived and battered into it.

When the door didn't give they started to tear at the timber with their hands and nails. Tor had once seen a beaver at work on the base of a tree, and these showed some of the same frenzied approach to the job. Sawdust flew in a cloud. Tor threw another spear that went through the shoulder of one of them at the neck and out the back in a welter of gore. The beast wailed, but kept working on the door with the others.

And we have used up all of the oil.

"More spears," Tor called. "Fetch spears. We have only moments before they break through."

Tor had turned slightly away, so almost did not notice the white flash as another *Alma* came out of the forest and ran, not towards the defenders, but to one of the outer huts. Even as Tor registered its presence it leaped onto the roundhouse roof and, in one bound, jumped across the space to the stockade wall, a distance of ten yards and more in a single leap. For a second it seemed to hang in the air, arms outstretched for balance above its head, steam streaming behind it like wisps of gauze, pale eyes staring, almost bulging out of their sockets.

It hit the top of the wall with a thud that shook the whole structure, and almost fell backwards, but it caught the top with a huge hand and had enough strength to grab at the wood and pull itself up and over. It jumped down inside the stockade before any Viking had a chance to move.

"They have learned a new trick," Bjorn said.

"Aye," Tor replied. "And now others will try the same. Have spears at the ready. We cannot allow any more to succeed."

Screams from below them told Tor that the beast was already wreaking havoc among the men. He took a brand in one hand, his sword in another, and leaped off the wall to confront it.

The *Alma* had its back to him, but from the screams he knew it had already been busy.

He had hoped to take it by surprise, but while he was still five yards from the beast it turned towards him. It held a dripping leg in its hand. The limb had been roughly torn from a body at the hip and the broken bleeding body of a Viking lay screaming on the ground.

The *Alma* looked down at the screaming man and

clamped its free hand to its ear, as if the noise pained it. The man wailed, louder. With one stomp of its right foot the beast caved in the man's chest, bones bursting thorough flesh and clothing as the foot went all the way through and broke his spine with a crack. The screams were suddenly cut off as blood spurted in a fountain from his mouth then the Viking thankfully lay still.

"You shall pay for that," Tor said softly.

The beast pulled back its lips and smiled, showing a broken yellow tooth in the upper row.

Snaggletooth. We have met before.

It raised the Viking's bloody leg to its mouth and bit off a chunk of flesh bigger than Tor's clenched fist. Blood smeared all over the lower half of its face as it chewed, then swallowed.

It smiled again, and threw the rest of the leg like a hammer, straight at Tor. He swatted it aside with the sword, feeling the blow reverberate all the way up his arm where he hit exposed bone.

The beast had red marks on the fur from the wounds that had been inflicted on it earlier, but neither seemed to be slowing it down as it roared in his face and came forward.

Tor stood his ground.

He waved the blazing firebrand in its face, but if this one was afraid of the flame it didn't show it. It swatted the firebrand to one side with the back of its left hand and reached for Tor with the right. The brand fell to the ground and went out.

The *Alma* roared again and stretched for Tor. He sliced down hard with the sword, cutting deep into the beast's arm. It didn't slow, and swiped its other arm towards Tor's head. He only just ducked in time, and was off balance as he thrust for the *Alma*'s belly. The sword tip barely penetrated the skin as the beast backed off.

They circled each other, the beast more wary now. Once more it clenched and unclenched its hands, muscles bunching under the skin. On a Viking Tor would be able to gauge in the eyes when an attack was coming, but the pale glassy stare of the *Alma* gave nothing away.

It threw itself at him with no warning. Tor rolled aside just in time as razor sharp nails reached for his face. He came back up holding the brand again. There was no flame left in it.

But there is still heat.

He stepped inside another swing of the massive palm and thrust his sword deep into the *Alma's* side.

It roared in his face. He shifted the brand in his grip so that he was holding it near the still smouldering tip, and thrust forward, stabbing it into the beast's right eye.

The eye popped and thick bloody fluid ran down the cheek. Fur seared and the rank smell of burning hair stung in Tor's nasal passages. He stepped back and sliced at it backhand with the sword, opening the muscles across the stomach. Its guts poked out from a gaping wound, yet still it came on, roaring and wailing, huge hands swinging like clubs, trying to find Tor.

If any one blow hit, Tor knew he would be dead in seconds. He bobbed and weaved -- always keeping just out of reach. Blood poured from the beast's wounds, and Tor knew that if he only kept moving he could wear it down.

The beast seemed to sense the same thing. It stopped and stood still, staring at him. It bent on its haunches and roared then launched itself forward with all the strength it had left. But it was already tired and slow. Another sliced backhand blow took a bloody chunk out of the right hand side of its face. Blind in both eyes now it blundered, raging and screaming. Tor thrust almost the full length of the sword into the small of its back.

It was finally brought it to its knees.

Tor brought the sword down and cleaved its skull in two.

It fell, face down, steaming on the stockade floor.

Tor put a foot on the body and screamed his victory to the cold night sky.

22

Skald remembered to breathe.

He'd watched the whole thing from on high, held back from leaping down to help by four of the small people.

Tor now stood over the body of the beast he'd slain, sword raised above his head. Bjorn and the men on the walkway managed to drive the attacking beasts from the gate by using spears and dropping firebrands to the ground below. Two other *Alma* tried to leap from the outer huts, but they were despatched by Viking spears before they reached the stockade wall.

They have repelled another attack. Surely the beasts will retreat.

But the large male still stood on the shore, watching.

He raised his hands to his lips and *hooted* again, long and high like a horn calling in fog.

As one, the remaining *Alma,* twenty or more, ran forward in long loping strides. At first Skald thought this was the mindless attack that the Viking had expected the first time. But the beasts had another plan in mind.

They clambered atop the huts, and launched themselves through the air at the stockade, white ghosts flying silently in the night, too many for the Viking to stop.

Spears took five, six, seven down, but the rest hit the top of the wall and clambered over.

The Viking fell back into the stockade in disarray. Skald knew with a sinking heart that singly, hand to hand, the beasts would be more than a match for any one Viking.

Except for Tor.

They will be slaughtered.

He felt something rise inside him, a red wave that threatened to wash through and take him away. He pushed it down.

I need to stay in control. If the berserker takes me, I have no way of knowing whom I might hurt.

He dragged himself away from the small people, forcibly.

"Go away," he shouted. "Please. I do not want to hurt *you.*"

This time they did not hold him back. Indeed they pulled away from him again, and once more there was fear in their eyes that disgusted Skald at having caused it.

He drew his long knife, grabbed his staff tightly, and was ready to head for the cliff path. Before he had gone a step Baren tugged at him.

"Please," he said softly, aware that the rage was close now. "Let me go. They need me."

Even as he said it, he realised that it wasn't true.

I need to do it. For me, not for them.

He pushed past Baren. She did not try to stop him. She grabbed the knife and took it from him. She put something else in his hand, something heavy.

Looking down, he saw a stone hammer, with a long thick wooden shaft and a leather strap as a support for the wrist. The stone at the end was the size of two large clenched fists and had been worked such that it could be used as a hammer on either side. The weight of it felt reassuring in his hand.

Better than that, it felt natural.

It felt *Viking.*

Baren once more did her impression of an *Alma.* Then she rapped him on the forehead with her knuckles, between the eyes, pointed at the hammer, then down to the scene below. Following her finger,

Skald saw she pointed directly at the large male who stood on the shore.

The best place to hit him. And the hammer is the best weapon, for me at least.

Skald nodded, then turned away. He left the ledge and headed down the slope as fast as he could manage, throwing caution to the wind as wild screams rose from within the stockade.

23

"To me," **Tor** called as the beasts jumped down from the wall into the stockade. "Viking, to me. Form a circle."

Bjorn was first to comply, bringing two burning firebrands with him and handing one of them to Tor. The rest of the Viking, even Kai and his henchmen, were quick to follow. They packed themselves as tight as they dared in a circle near the gate, yet still giving each other room to swing a sword arm.

"Hold fast men," Tor said. "We have killed many of these beasts already this night, and we shall send many more to join them. Hold the circle, and we will come through this."

One lad, Petr Axelsson, was tardy in joining them. Petr was, like Tor, on his first Viking. Back in Ormsdale he had been the tallest, the strongest lad of his age, and had regularly bested Tor on the fighting ground on which they trained. He had the strongest arm that had been seen in the community since Per himself had been coming of age.

It is not his arm he has need of now. It is his heart.

Petr stood in a bare patch of ground some twenty yards from the rest of the Viking. Fear had him in its grip and he could barely lift his sword for the trembling that coursed through his body. Hot piss ran from his breeches to puddle at his feet, and he whimpered, like a dog with a brutal master, a dog that knows a skelp is coming.

"Petr," Tor called. "To me. To the circle."

But there was no reply.

Tor stepped forward, but Bjorn pulled him back.

"Stay in the circle lad," the sail-master said. "'Tis our only hope."

"But Petr is in need of aid." Tor said.

Bjorn shook his head.

"It is too late for him. We have the rest of the men here to worry about now."

Tor saw that Bjorn was right. The closest *Alma* loomed over Petr. The Viking did not even raise his sword as the beast lifted him up in one huge hand.

Petr screamed. Tor had heard nothing like it since the night of Skald's accident, when they had reset the big bone in his friend's thigh. But even that had not held the same air of utter finality that he heard now. It was the scream of a man who knew he was doomed, and it chilled Tor to the bone.

The *Alma* opened its mouth wide and clamped teeth into the boy's face and skull, one long tooth going through the lad's cheek like a knife into an apple. It bit down and Petr's head caved in, blood and brains and bone running down the *Alma's* chest.

It *sucked* hungrily. It was the most obscene sound Tor had ever heard, and it seemed to go on forever. All round him Viking involuntarily cried out, and from somewhere across the circle came the noise, and smell, of violent retching.

Only when the beast was sated did it drop the body, a lifeless bundle of rags and bone that was half of what the lad had been in size. The beast shook its head violently from side to side and flecks of blood and brain flew in the air like water off a wet dog.

"We cannot fight such as these," someone called out. All around the circle men lowered their weapons, and one man broke off and ran, heading for one of the roundhouses.

He never made it. An *Alma* leaped on him, grabbed him close and squeezed. Blood spurted from mouth nose and ears. His rib cage gave way and he collapsed inwards like a squashed pillow. The *Alma* threw the body back. It landed at Tor's feet, no longer recognisable as having once been a man.

The Viking grouped together tightly, the circle closing once more.

"Steady," Tor called. "Remember men. You are Viking. If we are to die this night, we shall die like Viking."

The group of *Alma* closed in fast. They came on like trained fighters, light on their feet, almost loping, frost-white eyes fixed on their targets, hot breath steaming in the cold night air, hands curling and uncurling as they flexed their muscles. As one they roared.

The stockade suddenly filled with thunder.

"Stand firm," Tor called.

Bjorn stood by his left hand.

"If you get to Valhalla afore me lad, save me some ale."

"Only if Per has not finished it already," Tor laughed.

Then the beasts were on them.

Tor's sword took the first through the neck even as it reached for him, almost taking off the head. Hot blood spurted from the wound and hissed as it hit the firebrand, but the flame held steady. More blood splashed on Tor, on his helm, his cloak and his leggings. He felt the heat of it as it steamed in the night air.

As it fell the beast's body created a temporary barrier that the others would have to step over to reach him. Bjorn sent a second beast down on top of the first that had a wound from neck to groin. It spilled its guts at their feet as it fell and the smell stung in Tor's nostrils. Breathing through the mouth didn't help much.

"Are you sure Per is dead?" Bjorn said. "For surely he has just farted."

Tor smiled grimly.

Around them *Alma* tried to reach the Viking, but spear and sword were making a ring of iron that they couldn't penetrate. Tor and Bjorn were able to stand behind the dead beasts at their feet and fend off the others behind with the firebrands and the cold iron of their swords. The Viking to their left had the same idea, and as more *Alma* fell, so the pile of bodies grew higher, and their chance of defence grew.

Another beast stretched for Tor but it had to reach far forward and he was easily able to slice at the arms, once, twice, cutting through to bone both times. As it tried to back away the beast was pushed forward by the weight of other *Alma* behind it, and Tor cleaved its skull with a heavy downward blow. It fell on his face in front of him, and an idea suddenly hit him. He set its mane alight with the firebrand, and had to retreat a step as the beast burned.

He had earned himself and Bjorn a few seconds of respite and they were able to stand back as the other *Alma* stayed well away from the flames. But all too soon the fire died. Through the smoke they saw the beasts come forward again. Bjorn and Tor stood their ground, and sent another two beasts down to join the smoking pile.

But it did not go as well elsewhere.

A stretch of the circle to Tor's right buckled as a man went down under the force of a blow from a huge hand, three new red furrows running down his face from forehead to chin. Three *Alma* immediately leapt forward into the gap, swinging their arms like clubs, knocking the defenders aside as if they were no more than kindling for a fire.

Tor thrust his sword down the throat of the nearest beast to him, feeling the vibration all the way up his arm as teeth bit down on the iron. He pushed harder and the point exited at the back of the *Alma*'s neck in a bloody spray. He tugged the sword free and the beast's head lolled sideways, taken near clean off. Satisfied it was too near death to attack again, Tor turned to his left.

"Can you hold them here?" he said to the sail-master. "We must get the circle reformed or we are doomed.

The older man had a livid red scar running from his brow down his right cheek that crossed over his eye ridge, but the eye below still stared at him, blue and clear.

"We will hold. For as long as is needed."

Tor nodded, and leapt into the affray to his right, sword singing and flashing. Everywhere he struck gouts of blood flew. He took an *Alma's* arm clean off with one stroke, and an instant later thrust his blade into the groin of another, ripping up to its sternum.

His action gave the Viking behind him time to regroup. He cut at another *Alma* and missed his stroke, slipping to one knee in a puddle of slush and gore. But there was a man behind him ready with a spear to thrust it forward, taking the beast in the chest. That slowed the *Alma* down enough to allow Tor to step back into the circle of iron and flame.

All around, the battle ebbed and flowed. *Alma* fell, but there always seemed to be more in the ranks behind, and Tor felt the weight of his blade drag at his muscles and bring the first twinge of complaint.

We will not last much longer.

24

Skald arrived at the shore out of breath and with fresh pain shooting the whole length of his leg, spasms threatening to have it give way under him with every step. Only his will kept him going forward -- that, and the noise of battle from within the stockade.

He knew that there was little he could do in the kind of melee that was going on in there.

But I can distract the big male. That I can do.

His plan was simple. Attack the male, and stop it directing the efforts of the other *Alma.* Beyond that, he hadn't had time to think. If he did slow down, he was afraid that the futility of what he was about to attempt might become painfully obvious, and that he would lose what little resolve he had. He kept his eyes straight ahead.

The *Alma* watched him coming along the shore. It let him get within ten yards, then roared a battle cry at him.

Skald stood his ground and raised the hammer above his head. Using all of his experience of shouting over drunken Viking in the Great Hall, he *roared* back at it.

It stared at him, and Skald almost laughed at the puzzled expression on its face.

It took a step forward.

Skald took a step forward.

It stood up to its full height and beat rapidly at its chest with the palms of its hands, the noise echoing in the hills above like distant drumbeats.

Skald hit the hammer against his staff in a fast pounding rhythm.

Again it stood still, studying him, wary now.

It took another step forward.

Skald matched it.

He was now almost within reach of the beast's huge arms, and could smell the damp fur, like Per's dogs after a walk in the rain. Its breath steamed when it breathed. It shot an exhalation out through its huge nostrils, twin plumes rising upwards from them. Then it drew back its lips and smiled at him. It fell into a crouch and swayed from side to side.

Skald was painfully aware of the noises of battle behind him.

This is not working. If you do not do something, they will all die.

"You first," he said to the *Alma*.

It tensed its muscles and sprang at him. Skald had been waiting for it. He leaned back and, with as much strength as he could muster, threw the stone hammer at the creature's head.

His aim was true. With a dull *thud*, the hammer hit it right between the eyes. The beast fell in a heap at his feet and Skald screamed his victory to the night.

But he had celebrated too soon.

The beast wasn't fully unconscious. It threw out a massive hand and grabbed Skald by the left leg, dragging him to the ground beside it. Skald felt its nails pierce his flesh. There was a flush of wet warmth as blood ran inside his breeches.

He tried to roll away, stretching, trying to reach for the shaft of the hammer with his right hand. It was just beyond his fingertips, and even as he thought he just *might* reach it, the beast dragged him back again.

The beast lifted its head. It was groggy, and its huge tongue lolled out of its mouth, dribbling ropy drool on the ground. Skald kicked out at its face with his good leg, and again, but the hand that had him gripped tighter around his leg and pulled.

The beast was now coming around. It shook its

head and *rumbled* deep in its chest, then looked up, its eyes finding Skald.

It stared into his face. The mouth opened, and the tongue sunk back inside. Its lips turned back, revealing yellow fang-like teeth as long as Skald's fingers. He felt its hot breath on his face as it panted, then lunged for him.

Skald instinctively brought up his left hand, just as the beast bit down. Teeth met the wood of his staff, and splinters flew. The beast twisted its head violently from side to side, wrenching the staff from Skald's grasp and spitting it away. Its head came up again, mouth open wide. It bellowed straight in Skald's face.

Without warning, the red rage came on him. The last he remembered before it washed away all thought like a wave was reaching for the beast's head with his hands.

25

Tor cut at the reaching arm of an *Alma* and took the hand off at the wrist, having to close his mouth to stop it being filled with hot gushing blood. The beast barely slowed, and even when he thrust a blazing firebrand into its mane, setting its whole upper torso aflame, still it came forward. It was only stilled when Bjorn joined him and they both thrust their swords into the wide chest. Even as it fell it reached for them with the bloody stump.

Bjorn spat on the body.

"Stay down you devil."

Tor thrust his sword through the chest, just to make sure. He looked up, expecting another beast to be right behind, but there was none there. He caught a glimpse of white as a beast retreated back over the stockade wall and realised that it was the last of them to go.

We have beaten them.

Dazed Viking stood and looked at each other, as if surprised to be still alive.

They would not just depart. They were close to finishing us.

Something else has happened.

He broke the circle and sprinted for the walkway, taking the crude steps two at a time.

The *Alma* retreated towards the shore. The large beast that had led them rolled on the ground, struggling with something that clung to it and tore at its face with fingers hooked like claws. At first Tor thought it might be one of the small people from the cave, but when the attacker raised his head and howled Tor knew him straight away.

Skald!

A berserker is on him.

Tor jumped over the stockade wall, falling heavily on the other side but rising in almost the same movement. Behind him Bjorn called out, but Tor paid him no mind. All his attention was on Skald and the beast.

The beast prised Skald away from its face and managed to stand, groggily at first, then with more assurance. It held Skald at arm's length as the man screamed in its face, spittle flying, hands flailing, trying to reach the beast's eyes.

The *Alma* studied Skald for tow heartbeats, then lifted a hand to strike.

Tor was too far away to do anything, too far to try to throw his sword.

Skald!" he shouted, and tried to run faster, but he knew he was too late.

One skelp from that hand, and the Skald will be dead and gone forever.

The hand came up, and Tor flinched. But when it came down it was merely to give Skald a tap. It was enough to jerk his head sideways and make him slump unconscious in the beast's arms. The beast stroked Skald's head, almost tenderly, then turned towards the forest. It hooted, three times, and the remaining *Alma* followed.

No!

Tor screamed as he covered the ground between them. As he approached he raised his sword, but the beast turned, and Tor had to divert the killing stroke for fear of hitting Skald.

Almost contemptuously the beast backhanded Tor away.

It felt like being kicked by a carthorse. He flew, feet completely off the ground, a bundle of flailing limbs, hitting a tree, hard. Grey seeped in at the edges of his sight.

The last he saw before darkness took him down and away was the beast walking into the forest, the limp figure of Skald hanging in one huge hand.

26

When Skald came out of the wyrd he thought he must be back on the longboat, and in a storm at that, for he seemed to be lurching up and down and from side to side, so much so that his guts churned and he tasted acid in his mouth. He had suffered the effects of the sea more than enough in the past month to know the symptoms.

But the boat never smelled like this.

Something warm had him in a grip round the waist, and once more he smelled damp fur. He half-turned his head and looked directly at a wall of white hairs mere inches from his face. That was all he could see, but the smell was a lot stronger now, and he needed to turn away, else he might throw up.

Turning the other way, he looked down at the ground. He could just see it in the moonlight; enough to know it was passing by at a dizzying rate. Once more his insides churned. He closed his eyes, and it helped a little.

He had no memory of how he got here.

Wherever here is.

A beast had him, he knew that much. But the last thing he remembered was facing the large male on the shore and *roaring* at it. Now he felt as if he'd been awake for days without sleep or food, but with no memory of what he'd been doing in that time.

It has happened again. I am Berserker.

He wondered why he was still alive. Indeed, he seemed to have no major injuries. His leg hurt, but that was an old story that he was well used to.

But why would the beast take me alive?

He could think of several possibilities, and they all filled him with creeping dread. He considered trying to escape, but he had no weapon – his knife was with the small people, and where the hammer had fallen only Odin would know. His hands were pinned to his sides. When he tried to squirm free the beast merely gripped him tighter and he was forced to keep still if he wanted to breathe.

He felt tired and worn out, as if he had raced Tor up a hill and down again. His mind was full of questions that he could not answer and there was no escaping the clutch of the beast that carried him.

Rather than try, he let the tiredness take him.

Held in the hands of an *Alma*, being carried ever further from any hope of a rescue, Orjan Skald fell into a sound, almost peaceful, sleep.

27

When Tor woke he had to squint against bright rays of sunshine that threatened to lance straight through his head. It seemed that every muscle in his body hurt. He was sitting upright, the floor beneath him seeping cold through his breeches.

Where am I?

He tried to move, to push himself up to stand, but his arms refused to obey. At first he thought he might have been struck immobile, back broken by the blow dealt by the beast. The memory came back to him, of the *Alma*, walking silently into the forest, Skald hanging limply in its hand.

Skald!

Once again he tried to stand. But when he twisted, he realised he was bound, tied firmly to a post. As his eyes adjusted he found that he was inside one of the roundhouses.

Kai stood in front of him. He was wearing the wolf cloak and had his father's sword belted to his waist in the leather scabbard.

He saw that Tor was awake. He aimed a kick that caught Tor in the ribs and brought searing pain all down that side.

"Welcome back pup," Kai said. "As you can see, I have recovered what is rightfully mine."

Tor spat, tasting blood in his mouth.

"It would look better on you if you had earned it."

Kai punched Tor on the left side of his face and blood few along with a spray of spittle. Tor felt with his tongue. Two teeth had been loosened and once more he had the taste of blood in his mouth.

He spat a wad of it in Kai's face.

"Is that all you have? I know you are a coward but I

did not know you were also a woman."

Kai hit him again, and once more darkness started to creep around him.

I will not give him the satisfaction.

He forced himself to stay conscious. He heard a rasp as Kai unsheathed the sword. When his eyes focussed he saw the man standing above him, weapon raised.

He ignored it.

"Did you send men after the Skald?"

Kai laughed and lowered the sword.

"Send someone after *your* pet? Why would I do that?"

"He is Viking. We do not leave our men if they live."

Kai smiled as he sheathed the sword.

"The Skald is most certainly *not* alive," he said. "You saw it yourself. The beast carried him off."

Tor strained at the ropes that bound him.

"Then we must follow."

"There will be no following. The only place you will go is back to Ormsdale, to stand in the Great Hall and answer for your disloyalty to your rightful Captain. The sail-master will have a boat for me on the morrow, and we shall be on our way immediately."

Tor spat more blood.

"Viking do not run from a fight."

Kai smacked him hard on the jaw and Tor's head rang.

"There *is* no fight," Kai said. "Twenty and more of those beasts lie dead in the snow out there and the rest have fled. I shall take their furs and heads back to the Thane as geld. We shall at least have something from this journey."

Tor smiled, remembering.

"What if I told you we could have much more?" he said. "What if I spoke of a mine, where silver is abundant?"

Kai hit him hard again, and this time when he spat a tooth went with it. But still he smiled.

"There is no such mine," Kai said.

Tor grinned through the blood.

"Have a look in yonder cave," he said. "There is a map carved there. A map that will lead you to untold treasure."

He saw the greed in Kai's eyes, a greed that had always been there, even when both were boys.

I have him.

"If you lie, I will have you killed," Kai said.

Tor laughed at him.

"I am shitting in my breeks at the thought. Go and look at the cave wall. I speak the truth."

Kai left. As he went through the doorway Tor finally allowed himself to drop his head. After a time his ears stopped ringing and he felt he might be able to move without throwing up. He strained at the ropes that bound him to the post, but they had been tied so tight he had scarcely any room for movement. Rough leather chafed at his wrists. He tugged and pulled until the pain got too great, but he could not get loose.

He called out, but no one answered.

The ground was freezing beneath him and he felt the cold seep up through to his very bones.

If I do not get up from here soon it will be a block of ice they take back to Ormsdale.

His ribs ached where the *Alma* hit him, and the side of his face felt swollen where Kai punched him. But his anger kept all thoughts of pain away. That, and the thought of Skald in the hands of the beasts.

Kai returned ten minutes later. He did not waste time getting to the point.

"This silver of which you spoke? How do you know it is there?"

"If I tell you, will you free me?"

"Tell me, and I will consider it."

I doubt that very much. But it is my only chance.

"The small people gave Skald a pendant," Tor said. "Why do you not ask them?"

Kai snorted.

"I would if it were possible. They have all gone."

"All?"

Kai nodded.

"The cave was empty save for a few furs. There was nothing that could be of any value."

Tor spat more blood.

"You saw the map?" he said.

Kai nodded.

"And you believe me about the mine?"

"Aye," Kai said. "We found two more of the silver amulets in one of the houses. But it will do *you* no good. I will take most of the men with me, but you shall stay here until our return."

Tor strained at his bonds, raging, but the tethers held firm.

"Skald is my friend. I must go after him," he shouted.

Kai slapped him again, hard, across the cheek.

"You must do as your Captain commands," he said. He spat in Tor's face. "And your Captain says stay. *You* are *my* pet now."

Kai left again. A few minutes later Tor heard the sounds of him barking orders and men preparing to leave. But no one came to talk to him, and the cold seeped ever further into his bones.

It was several hours after Kai and the men left before anyone came in to the roundhouse. Tor only knew that men had been left behind by the sound of axe against wood coming from somewhere outside, but when he called out, no one replied, and no one came near him. He drifted in and out of consciousness, but in both places he kept seeing the same thing, Skald, limp and unmoving, being carried into the forest by the *Alma.*

He roused himself by kicking his legs up and down to try to get some life into them, but even that act drained him. The cold gripped him so tight that he was near ready to give himself to it.

He was barely able to lift his head when Bjorn the sail-master walked through the doorway.

"Help me," Tor managed to whisper.

Bjorn cut his bonds and half-dragged, half-carried him to a straw bed, where he laid Tor down and covered him with furs. Tor lay there, shivering, while Bjorn lit a fire in the stone grate.

"I am sorry lad," the sail-master said. "I had to make sure the cur was well gone before coming to your aid."

Tor's teeth chattered too much for him to reply. Bjorn left him lying there wondering if he would ever be warm again.

The sail-master returned with a bowl of fish stew. It tasted as foul as ever, but its heat did its job, and Tor began to feel as if he *might* just live a while longer.

Bjorn spoke while Tor ate.

"We thought you were dead when we got to you under yon tree," he said. "That was some skelp the beast gave you."

Tor felt at his ribs. None seemed broken, but there was a large area that hurt to the touch. He opened his jerkin to check, and closed it again quickly. A purple bruise covered his side from nipple to hip.

"I will live. I shall be stiff for days," he replied. "But I am well enough for what must be done."

He stood, too fast, and the room spun around him, as if he had drank a bucket full of mead. He had to swallow to keep the stew from coming up. He sat again, hard.

"Take it slowly lad," Bjorn said, putting out a hand to stop Tor from toppling backward. "You look as close to death as any man I have seen these last few days."

Tor sat and ate more of the stew, this time allowing it to do its job. Bjorn told him the rest of what he had missed.

"There has been no sign of the Skald," he began. He put a hand on Tor's shoulder. "I am sorry lad. And we lost six other men in the fight. But Kai is not concerned with even giving them a burial. He has four of us working on the boat. The rest he has taken with him, in search of your silver."

Tor stood again, slower this time. The room stayed still and he no longer felt nauseous. He was still as weak as a newborn, but he felt stronger with every passing minute.

"I shall go after him. Or rather, I shall go after Skald. I cannot leave him in the hands of those things."

Bjorn put a hand on Tor's shoulder.

"The Skald is surely dead and gone. It is a fool's quest you undertake."

Tor shook his head.

"He lives yet. I feel it, here." He thumped at his chest, and immediately regretted it as pain shot up his side and he coughed, tasting blood.

"I shall come with you," Bjorn said.

Tor pushed him away.

"Nay, you must finish the boat. We may have need of a means to escape quickly."

"You cannot do this alone. Not in the state you are in."

Tor smiled grimly.

"I have found myself to be capable of more than I though possible these past days," he said. "I will endure."

Bjorn smiled back at him.

"I believe you might lad." He sighed. "I shall do as you ask. I shall build you a boat. It will not be a longboat, nor will it be suited for war, but it will suffice to get us home."

"That is all I ask," Tor said quietly.

But at that moment, the Halls of Ormsdale seemed very far away indeed.

Ten minutes later Tor said his goodbye to Bjorn at the gate of the stockade.

"The beasts may return at nightfall," Tor said.

"Do not worry lad," Bjorn replied. "I shall not make the same mistake as Kai. Long before the sun goes down we shall be up in yonder cave with a roaring fire going. And on the morrow, we shall have a boat, and will anchor well away from the land. Even if these beasts can swim, we shall see them coming from afar. Do not worry about us."

"If Kai returns before me, things may go bad for you," Tor said. "You should say I tricked you."

Bjorn smiled.

"If Kai returns before you, I may deal with him myself. Now go. You have a Viking to find. May the Gods go with you." They clasped hands, and Tor set off across the shore.

Something caught his eye among the stones. Looking down, he found Skald's staff and a hammer with a stone head. He put the hammer in the shoulder pack he carried, and carried the staff in his left hand.

He waved back, once, to where Bjorn stood, then walked into the forest.

He had wanted to leave immediately, but Bjorn had insisted he took some minutes to prepare for a journey. Now that he was within the forest, he was glad he had taken the time.

He pulled a cloak around his chest. Underneath it he wore a leather jerkin and two pairs of heavy coarse woollen breeks. They had belonged to Viking who perished the previous night. He also wore fur-lined deerskin mittens and boots, and he had found a sword. It had been badly notched, and wasn't anywhere near as well balanced as Per's. It was also much shorter, having been broken and reshaped at some time in the past. It was more suited for close work than the longer weapon he'd used so effectively the night before.

But it is a sword nonetheless. It will kill as well as any.

His helm proved to be too battered to rescue, but he found a worthy replacement that was made of thick leather with iron studs woven into the material, and a chinstrap to pull it down over his ears. He had to wash some bone and brain from inside it, and he tried not to think of the Viking who had so recently worn it as he pulled it over his hair, letting the long strands fall out at the back.

He carried some dried fish and a skin of water in a shoulder bag, which felt heavy now that they had been joined by the stone hammer. The sword swung at his side on a thick belt and he used Skald's staff to push through the snow that was much thicker here under the trees, and getting steadily deeper as he headed away from the shore.

He followed a set of large tracks, much bigger than any man would make, and twice he found scat that was still warm and reassured him he was on the right trail.

There was no sign of Kai having been this way, but Tor guessed that the *Alma* might know routes that did not appear on any map. He kept his eyes on the tracks and followed them as they led him high up onto the mountainside above the settlement.

Be well Skald. I am coming.

28

The beast carried Skald high up into the mountain passes above a long wide glacial plain. All night and most of the morning it had strode, faster than a Viking could have ran.

Skald felt light headed and nauseous. He dry-heaved but nothing came up. The yawing and rolling continued as they went almost straight up a mountainside, with Skald looking down at dizzying vistas of forest and glacier below them.

He remembered the glacial plain from the map back in the cave. Somewhere above them, if the relief had shown true, there would be massive stone buildings, and a statue that terrified Skald greatly.

Even the thought of it brought the wyrd rushing into his mind. He fell inside, grateful for the escape.

He floated high above the same glacial plane. Two men walked there seemingly impervious to the biting wind and snow that blew horizontally down the valley. One man was short, dark skinned and with a quick smile that was betrayed by a certain cunning behind his eyes. The other was tall, broad shouldered, and carried a stone hammer that Skald would not even have been able to lift never mind wield.

Skald realised these were not men he was being shown.

These were Gods.

Thor and Loki were on a mission, and he knew what it was, for the old story rushed back into his mind, the wyrd showing him something he had otherwise forgotten, one the many tales a Skald had to learn before he was allowed to stand in the Great Hall.

Odin sent them to the ice-lands, sent them to undo a

great wrong that Loki had wrought. Years before, Loki had congress with a giantess, one of the old Jotun, and the union produced a male child called Varni. The giantess died in birthing him, and Odin, taking pity, allowed the boy a place in the halls of Asgard.

And things went well, for a while, but the child could not contain his heritage for long. Indeed, many of the Gods were afeared of him, for he grew exceeding large, and the time soon came when they looked for an excuse to be rid of him.

They got their chance one night in Valhalla when Varni got drunk on mead and ale. He abused the Gods, bewailing his plight as neither one thing nor the other, and would not be silenced.

The Gods chased him out of Asgard and he ran amok through the length and breadth of Midgard. Wherever he passed, he left death and destruction in his wake. Eventually the wailing of the people reached back to Asgard itself, and Odin heard.

Odin sent Loki after Varni, and sent Thor with him, to ensure the trickster complied with his wishes. They travelled long and far, and had many adventures on the journey, but finally Thor and Loki found Varni, gathering followers to him in a great temple high up in the mountains. He had built great halls of stone -- halls he could call his own, halls to rival those of Asgard itself. And he had made for himself followers, hairy beasts that would dance for him and do his bidding. He set the beasts against the Gods and a great battle was fought. Thor and Loki smote many until all that remained were the Gods themselves.

Thor battled the giant for six days and nights, until finally with one great blow of the hammer Molnjir he hit the giant between the eyes.

It is told that the whole of Midgard shook as the giant fell.

They bound Varni in his temple, lashing him to long slabs of rock. And as Thor and Loki stood back, the ropes became as hard as iron, binding the giant in place. And Varni cursed them, promising Ragnarok, the end of Gods, if he should ever get free. But the Gods were deaf to his curses, even as the stone took him, becoming one with his flesh, binding him there.

And there they left him, high in the mountain fastness, with only the wind and the cold for comfort.

But Varni is not dead, only sleeping.

In his dreams, he calls out for aid.

And sometimes, he is answered.

29

Tor followed the tracks for most of the morning and into the early afternoon until they climbed up out of the forest and onto a long glacial plain. He had run most of the way. His breath came hot and heavy, and the bruises from the earlier beatings throbbed in time with his heartbeat.

The ice field stretched away into the blue misty distance. He stopped on the edge of the glacier and leaned heavily on Skald's staff. Despite the cold he sweated profusely, especially under the woollen breeks. He took the water sack from his bag and sipped at it. He did not take a lot, for he did not know how much further he might have to run.

And now that he had lost the trail he only had a vague idea of the direction he needed to take. He remembered the map on the cave wall, and the depiction of the long glacier where he now stood. His objective was somewhere in the misty distance, ten miles or more across the ice.

He placed a hand above his eyes, trying to cut out the glare of the sun. There was a darker spot; far out on the glacier, several miles away, but from this distance he could not make out what it was. But it was the only thing of note on the white plain, so he set his gaze on it, and started off.

The going was slower now. The ice proved to be treacherous, with many crevasses and chasms studded along its length. Several times he had to retrace his steps after his path led him only to a gully too deep or too wide to cross. Occasionally he would catch glimpses of the darker patch on the ice, and as he got closer, he could see that it was not one, but several dark masses. Almost an hour later he realised that the darker patches were in fact bodies.

It did not look like any of them were moving.

As he got closer still he saw streaks of red on the snow, and walked faster, only slowing when he got within twenty yards of the first body.

There were four Viking lying in puddles of their own gore, and three Alma, just as dead alongside, cut with many sword strokes. Of Kai and the other Viking who left with him there was no sign, but a scattering of weapons on the snow showed that most, if not all of them, had been disarmed before whatever had happened to them.

Among the discarded weapons Tor found Per's woven leather scabbard and, just to one side of it, the long sword. It had been bent almost double in the middle, as if someone of great strength had grabbed at both ends and *twisted*. Other weapons had suffered the same fate, swords, spears, and even several hunting knives.

The Alma have them. Odin help them, the Alma have them.

One of the bodies surprised him by letting out a groan of pain. Tor ran to the man's side. When he bent he was amazed that the man still lived. He had been opened from groin to chest, and his guts spilled over onto the ice where they had already started to freeze.

"What happened here," Tor asked.

"Snowbeasts," the man said, his voice barely a whisper. "Surprised us."

He coughed, and grabbed at Tor's arm, squeezing until pain receded enough that he was once more able to speak.

"Some of us fought. Killed one myself. Cut its balls off," he said, and tried to laugh but only brought himself more pain.

"Kai," the man whispered.

"What about Kai?"

The man's eyes went cold as flint.

"Coward," he managed to say. "Surrendered."

Surrender? Not even Kai would stoop so low.

Tor would have asked more, but the man's eyelids fluttered, the eyes underneath rolling up in their sockets until only white showed and the Viking fell too deep in shock and pain to speak. All Tor could do was grasp his hand and hold it until the grip gave out and the Viking's head lolled forward on his chest.

Tor stood head bowed, and asked the God's favour in granting the Viking admittance to Valhalla. But he had no time for the proper ceremony. A trail of blood spots led away to the north, heading up the length of the glacier to the high peaks.

Tor followed at a run.

30

Skald kept his eyes tightly closed. The beast climbed up a steep incline and, despite the fact it had Skald cradled in its arm, it moved fast and fleet of foot, finding holds instinctively and clambering up the cliff like a squirrel going up a tree.

Skald only opened his eyes when the sense of motion slowed, and the breeze that had been constantly on his face for many minutes slackened and died away.

At first he thought that night had fallen again, but as his eyes adjusted he realised he was being carried deep down into a cave. By turning and stretching his neck he could see the cave mouth, and blue sky beyond, receding quickly away from them.

A few seconds later the air cleared again and he once more felt a breeze on his face, but this one was slightly warm, and smelled, a smell he was getting to know. It smelled of *Alma.*

It wasn't quite dark here and light, soft, almost dusty, snowflakes filtered through from somewhere high above. The cave had opened out to a wide cavern and even from his limited viewpoint Skald saw that they walked among high buildings carved deep into the stone walls, turrets, windows and staircases speaking of an abode of men.

Or giants.

Pale eyes watched their passage, many pairs of them, back in the shadows in the buildings.

Finally the beast stopped. It dropped Skald to the ground, and he was surprised not to hit rock, but a carpet of dried moss and ferns. It took him long seconds to get his bearings. He had got accustomed to travelling in that long loping gait and his vision swam slightly, still keeping time with the rhythm of the beast's stride. He knew from experience on the longboats after a spell in rough seas that it would take hours for that to settle.

His legs wobbled, not believing they were on solid ground, and the left one refused to take his weight at first. He had to lock it out at the knee to stand upright.

When he finally felt stable and looked round he nearly fell back to the moss.

He had been dropped on a high flat platform with a view down over the length of the cavern. The buildings and streets were much more extensive than he had previously imagined; high vaulted edifices of grey, almost black stone curving away into the gloom above and burrowing down into darkness far below. Several had crumbled, piles of stone at their base attesting to their ages old ruination, but enough remained for Skald to see the splendour there had once been.

But all glory was long since passed. An aura of decrepitude hung over the stones. Where once Gods may have walked this cavern, the streets were now given over to moss and fern, rubble and dust. And amid the rubble walked the Alma -- not as many as had been shown to him in the wyrd -- but more than enough to send a creeping fear up his spine.

Now that his eyes had become fully adjusted to the dim light he saw high piles of dried fern and moss perched on the rooftops of some of the buildings.

Nests. They make nests in high places.

Something moved behind him, a rustling amid the dry vegetation, and Skald suddenly realised where he was.

And I am in one of them.

He turned, and came face to face with an *Alma*.

It studied him curiously while he studied it.

This one was older than the others he'd seen -- much older. It sat on its haunches on a thick bed of ferns, and its body looked too large and corpulent to be able to stand for any length of time. Its chest was broad but somehow sunken and the fur, which on the rest had been white and sleek, was straggly and silvery-grey, with livid pink patches of skin showing through in thinner parts. Its whole face was almost black, wrinkled like tanned leather -- large, round and flat. Heavy lids hung half closed over white eyes sitting in shadow under heavy brows.

The large male that had carried Skald here stood to one side, head down and turned away from the old one.

It is showing respect. Respect for an elder?
Or respect for a leader?

Behind the old male a much smaller female groomed the thinning fur, occasionally picking a flea or mite from the body and crushing it between surprisingly flexible fingers. Something moved in the old one's lap. A small, white bundle of fur jumped away at the sight of Skald and hid between the legs of the female, pink eyes staring in fear at this new thing that had wakened it.

Skald watched the old male warily. He seemed to be in no immediate danger. The *Alma* still studied him, looking straight into his eyes. It reminded Skald of the way Per used to look at the boys when they were trying to hide some wrongdoing. Just as he could never stand under the Viking's stare, so it proved with the *Alma*. Skald broke his gaze first and looked away.

He considered running. He looked over the old beast's head, searching for an escape route, no matter how infeasible he knew the idea to be. He peered into the shadows at the far end of the cavern. It was dark there, but somehow he *knew* there was a presence there. The wyrd kicked in, not completely, just enough to overlay what he was seeing with an earlier vision.

Two columns of black stone dominate the far end of the cavern. Behind them, seemingly carved straight into the rock wall, sits a massive plinth, on which lies a giant effigy of a bound man, mouth wide open, screaming for eternity. Alma, dozens of them, carry screaming Viking through the chamber and sling their bodies onto the plinth. They tear open the still living bodies, coolly methodically, disembowelling tearing. Blood splatters on and around the plinth -- but most runs down the runnels towards the statue. And where the blood hits it, the stone begins to change, lightening in colour, softening, as it takes on texture, soaking up the blood, drinking it in.

The wyrd left him, and now he was merely looking at the darkness at the far end of the cavern. Two tall columns of black stone rose up into the gloom high above.

Skald could not see what lay behind them in the shadows.

But I know he is there.

Varni is there.

As the wyrd left Skald the old *Alma* was still looking in his eyes. It drew back its lips and hooted, laughing. It dragged itself to its feet on stunted legs and waddled grotesquely towards Skald.

He had nowhere to go, trapped by a sheer drop at his back. He stood as the beast reached out a hand, flinched as it touched the top of his head. The beast turned Skald's face so that once more they looked into each other's eyes.

Together, they fell into the wyrd.

31

The sun had started to set when Tor finally walked off the glacier and stood looking up at the almost sheer cliff above him. A few drops of blood on the snow were all that signified he was still on the right track.

But it is enough.

A snell wind blew across the face of the cliff, and from where he stood he could see few places that he might rest on the ascent. He felt as tired as he had ever been in his life, every muscle aching. He struggled even to hold on to the backpack, and knew there was no possibility he would make it even ten yards up the cliff without rest.

He walked along the foot of the cliff searching for a place to hide from the worst of the wind and found it minutes later, an overhang that wasn't deep enough to call a cave, but was big enough for him to crawl inside and sit upright. He arranged his cloak so that the bulk of it was underneath him, protecting him as much as it could from the cold. He jammed his body into a corner and tried to relax. The efforts of the day started to take their toll. His head lolled on his chest and he closed his eyes, ready to let the dreams come.

But even in his weariness, his thoughts would not let him sleep. His mind was full of fire and blood. He saw himself thrust Per's sword again, and again into the bodies of the Alma. He saw his sword cleave an *Alma's* skull. He smelled again the acrid stench as their fur burned. He heard the screams, of *Alma*, and of men. And always he came back to the one thing that had almost taken his courage from him.

An Alma looms over Petr Axelsson. It opens its mouth wide and clamps its teeth into the boy's face and skull, one tooth going through the lad's cheek like a knife into an apple. It bites down and the head caves in, blood and brains and bone running down the Alma's chest as it sucks the life from the boy.

That could be Skald. It might already be Skald.

He allowed himself an hour of rest before he resigned himself to the fact that sleep would not come. He still felt tired, but his muscles were now stiff rather than sore, and he knew from experience that they would loosen as soon as he started to exert himself again.

He was not worried about the lack of sleep – he had often spent several nights in a row without resting when hunting, whether for wolf or bear, and he knew his body's limits. He was getting close to them. But he could go on for some time yet.

And more still if it means I might rescue Orjan

It was full dark when he crawled out of his refuge, wincing at the bite of the wind against his face. The full moon lit the cliff in sharp relief, and just above his head he could see shadows marking cracks where he might make his first handhold. He tied Skald's staff to his shoulder bag. He hung the bag across both shoulders so that the weight was even distributed across his back and tentatively started his ascent.

The early stages went easier than he could have hoped. When he looked down after only ten minutes climbing, he had left the ice plain far below.

He found a ledge where he could get both feet on at once. The wind tried to pluck at his body, wanting to dash him away to the ground below. Tor leaned his body in against the cliff face; cheek pressed against the cold rock, and rested his arm muscles, letting some of the tension drain out of them. He stayed there for five minutes until he felt ready for the next step.

He had just started to raise his hands to feel for a

hold when a rattle of pebbles came down from above and brushed his cheek.

He looked up.

An *Alma* was coming down the cliff, swinging from handhold to handhold as easily as it would walk across a meadow. It looked down and saw that Tor had noticed it.

It roared its defiance. The noise rang off the cliff face like a bell.

The beast let go of its last hold.

It dropped like a stone, heading straight down on top of him.

32

It was daylight in the wyrd, and all was deathly quiet.

The ancient Alma held Skald's hand as they walked between two titanic black pillars and stood in front of a giant lying bound on the huge pedestal. This was no statue. For the first time Skald realised that Varni was not just a giant.

He was not of human form.

He was an Alma – of huge proportions, a thirty-foot beast, and he was bound tight to the stone by cords thicker than Skald's good leg.

Varni.

The giant's eyes opened. Pale, milky white, they looked straight at Skald. It opened its mouth, showing huge yellow teeth as long as Skald's forearm, and roared. Raging, the giant thrashed against its bonds.

I know that rage.

I have seen it, in the beasts.

I have felt it, in myself.

Like the Alma, Skald too had taken something from the Sleeping God.

And now the God took something from him. It looked into his mind, into the wyrd, and drew out something that Skald had seen earlier.

Alma, dozens of them, carried screaming Viking through the chamber and slung their bodies onto the plinth. They tore open the still living bodies, coolly methodically, disembowelling tearing. Blood splattered on and around the plinth...but most ran down the runnels towards the statue. And where the blood hit it, the stone began to change, lightening in colour, softening, as it took on the texture of hair and flesh, soaking up the blood, drinking it in.

Then came a roar.
White turned red as the drums beat a word into his skull.
Doom.

The old Alma by Skald's side hooted, laughing, and the God joined in, the laughter echoing up through the cavern and dislodging snow to fall like silver dust around them.

Skald came out of the wyrd with tears running down his cheeks.

Now he knows what needs to be done.

And finally Skald realised what the wyrd had been showing him this past month and more.

If there is doom here, I brought it with me.

There was a commotion across the cavern. *Alma* called and hooted, and the old beast beside Skald called back excitedly.

Skald looked down.

It was dark in the cave now, but there was enough light to see a group of snow-white *Alma* herd a party of around a dozen unarmed Viking through the streets.

The old *Alma* slapped the ground hard with his palms, drumming out a rhythm, and the *Alma* below chanted in time as they marched the Viking through the streets. Soon they were almost out of view and Skald had to lean perilously close to the edge of the drop to catch sight of them.

I have to know.
Is he there?
Is Tor there?

One of the Viking wore a tattered, bloodied, but instantly recognisable wolf cloak.

"Tor," Skald called.

But it was Kai who looked up. There was no

recognition in the man's eyes, just a dull resignation as he trudged with the others out of Skald's view. Skald started to walk forward, hoping to find a way off the nest, but the old *Alma* pushed him gently back to his original place. The tall male who had brought Skald here looked on, with an expression that Skald immediately recognised.

He'd seen it often enough in the Great Hall in Ormsdale.

Tor's pet they had called him there. Now it looked like the old *Alma* had claimed him, and he was not going to be allowed to leave.

33

Tor leaped sideways' grabbing for a handhold that looked barely large enough for his fingertips. His fingers gripped, then suddenly had to take his whole weight as his feet slipped off the edge. His shoulder muscles took the strain, complaining at the effort on already bruised muscles. He swung, almost falling, as the beast tumbled level with him. It threw out a hand and raked talons down Tor's shin, digging through the breeks and bringing a sharp pain that caused him to scream in agony.

Then the beast was past. Somewhere below he heard it scrambling for purchase on the rock.

Tor looked for a handhold that would get him moving upwards quickly, but there was nothing immediately in sight. Straining, he swung himself onto the narrow ledge he'd been on before. This time he had his back to the cliff and was able to look down.

The beast was twenty yards below. It had managed to halt its descent and was even now starting to come back towards Tor, roaring as it came.

Tor almost overbalanced as he drew the sword from his belt, and had to spend valuable seconds shifting the weight of the shoulder bag to stop it toppling him over.

By that time the beast was almost at his feet. Tor bent to get a sword stroke at it, and once more his balance was compromised. He teetered precariously as he swung.

The sword took the beast across the knuckles of one hand, raising a bloody welt. The beast stopped, a foot below Tor's feet, its eyes fixed on the weapon.

It roared again, and Tor saw all the way down its throat.

But it came no further towards him, staying just out of reach of the tip of the sword. Tor leaned down and swung again. The beast pulled back its lips and smiled as the weapon swished past, an inch from where it gripped the rock face.

Tor squirmed and, with his left hand, tried to free Skald's staff from where he'd tied it to the bag. His knot-work had been too good. The staff was bound tight to the handle of the bag. But just feeling the weight of the bag gave him another idea.

The beast watched warily as Tor eased the bag off his shoulders.

Tor nearly lost his balance twice, and once, when he'd taken his eye off the beast, it leapt forward in an attack.

He barely managed to fend it off with a swing of the sword. It was a lucky stroke, but it opened the *Alma's* cheek. It retreated back to its handhold beneath him, and this time when it smiled it was a lopsided thing, showing the yellow teeth all the way back to near its ear on the left hand side.

With much twisting and slow careful movements, Tor finally managed to free the bag. Holding one end of the staff he swung the other in a high arc. With the weight of the hammer inside aiding it, he brought the bag round to club the side of the *Alma's* head. The blow shifted the beast's centre of balance. Tor roared as it lost its handhold and started to fall. But his own centre of balance was far from secure, and when the bag kept swinging it pulled him to one side so that his feet came off the ledge. He tried to jam his sword into the rock, looking for a crack but he found none.

The sword hit stone and was wrenched from his hand. It tumbled away into the night.

Tor toppled over, falling on top of the Alma.

His weight sent them both tumbling down the cliff.

The wind roared in his ears and he grabbed and tore at anything he could find that might stop his headlong rush to the ice far below.

The *Alma* saved him. It found a hold with its right hand, just as Tor grabbed at its mane with his free hand. He wrapped the hand as firmly as he could in the long hair and held on tight. Both of them swung wildly, and Tor thought they might once more fall, but the *Alma* held, huge fingers wedged firmly in a crack in the rock, arm muscles bulging as it took the strain of both bodies on one arm.

It turned its face and roared at Tor, spraying a fine mist of blood from the bloody cheek. It squirmed and threw its body from side to side, trying to reach Tor with its left hand, but he hung almost directly behind it. The *Alma* could not get to him without using both hands.

They hang there for several seconds, then the beast surprised Tor by starting to climb, going up nearly as fast as they had come down.

And when we reach the top, I will have to face it without my sword.

34

Night had fallen outside, but Skald became aware that it was not completely dark inside the cavern. The walls themselves seemed to glow with a silver luminescence. Skald had seen something similar from weed in the water at night in the fjord at home.

Mayhap this is something similar. But I do not think I will be allowed to investigate.

The luminescence provided enough light for him to make out most of the cavern.

All the visible nests on the rooftops were now occupied by *Alma*, settling themselves down, like dogs creating a sleeping space. But escape wasn't going to be that easy. The old male showed no signs of sleep. It sat on the bed of ferns and never took its eyes off Skald. It *hooted* from time to time, lips drawn back in a smile, and drummed the flats of its palms on a patch of exposed stone. Skald wondered if it was quite sane.

Not that it will make any difference.

Skald's bad leg ached with a deep pain. He longed for his staff, but that was long gone. He was forced to sit, with the leg stretched out in front of him. He kneaded it, as if he was making bread, but the pain persisted, and indeed was getting worse.

If he were back in Ormsdale, or even on the longboat, he would have escaped into the wyrd, where there was no pain, for a while at least. But he could not do that here. All that waited in the wyrd in this place was the sleeping giant, and Skald was in no hurry to face that fury again.

The old *Alma* laughed again, as if it had heard Skald's thought.

And mayhap it did.

Skald remembered how easily the *Alma* had taken

them both into the wyrd. In all his time since the accident Skald had never been in the wyrd with another being, and now, in the space of a few days, he had done it twice, with Baren and now with the *Alma*. He suspected it was something to do with the sleeping giant and its desire for freedom and awakening.

He was very frightened that such an awakening was not too far from coming to pass.

And it will all be my fault.

35

The *Alma* sped up the cliff. Tor clung tightly to its mane, trying not to think what would happen if the hair came away in his hand. They passed close to the spot where his sword was still stuck in the crack in the rock, but Tor dared not try to reach it for fear of losing his already precarious position.

Up here the air was even colder, and he felt frost at his cheeks. He tried to wrap his hand even tighter in the mane. The shoulder bag still swung at the end of Skald's staff, and he clung tightly at the wood with his left hand.

If I lose that, I will have no chance at all.

The climb seemed to go on forever, and Tor's right arm and shoulder had gone almost completely numb. He locked out his muscles, but wasn't sure he would be able to hold for much longer.

He was thinking of a way to take the beast down to death with him when the *Alma* suddenly pulled them up onto a ledge.

Tor had just enough of his wits about him to roll off the back and scuttle to one side before the beast turned on him, roaring anger in his face.

He swung the staff in a wide arc. The shoulder bag was still accelerating as it smashed into the side of the *Alma*'s head. The cut on its face widened and blood poured down that side.

Tor almost cried out in triumph, but he had celebrated too soon. The beast grabbed at the bag, dragging it, and the staff, from Tor's hands. It ripped the bag in two and the contents -- a water bag, some dried fish and the stone hammer -- fell to the ground at its feet.

The *Alma* dropped into a crouch and launched

itself at Tor. He waited until the last possible instant and leaped to one side. The beast threw out an arm, but only caught the edge of Tor's cloak, ripping it from his back. The beast wasted seconds tearing the cloak to shreds, by which time Tor had rolled to where the bag had fallen. He retrieved the staff and the hammer, and when the beast turned its attention back to him he was ready for it. He swung the staff like a sword, and hit his mark, once more getting a blow in on the cut on the beast's face. The whole of that side of its face was now a pulpy red mass. It smiled through bloody gums, two teeth hanging loosely in their sockets.

The beast grabbed for the staff, but Tor was too fast for it, spinning and swinging the wood again at its head. This time when the beast grabbed for it Tor let go.

While the *Alma* spent time in tossing the staff to one side, Tor rolled forward beneath its belly and smashed the stone hammer into one of its knees, feeling bone crack and crumble. The beast howled and fell to one side, all strength gone in the injured leg.

Tor stood above it, and brought the hammer down once more. The *Alma* raised an arm in defence and the stone head struck it full on the elbow.

Bones cracked.

The beast howled again and tried to crawl away, all thought of fight forgotten. Tor leaped onto its back, grabbing the mane in his left hand and bringing the hammer down with his right. He hit the skull on the conical point at the back. His first stroke sent the beast to its knees. His second broke bone and tore scalp, punching through to the brain below. Blood gushed over Tor's face and he tasted it in his mouth. The beast jerked and bucked in its death throes as he brought the weapon down a third time. The stone head of the weapon went all the way through the beast's head to hit the rock beneath.

The beast finally went still, but Tor pounded, again and again, until his arm, red with gore all the way to the elbow, got too tired to lift the hammer.

He dropped the weapon and staggered over to the water skin, drinking deeply until he could no longer taste blood at his mouth. All the while he kept his eyes on the beast, appalled at the ruin he had made.

Slowly, his heart stopped pounding in his ears, and his blood calmed. For the first time since the beast pulled them onto the ledge he had time to look around. He stood at the mouth of a large cave, looking like a black empty maw in the dim light. A slight breeze came from inside, and it smelled, of *Alma.*

Tor walked over to the hammer and lifted it. It felt twice as heavy as it had before. He leant over Skald's staff and bent to pick it up. Nausea and tiredness hit him as much as if he had himself been hit by the hammer. He sat down, hard, bringing fresh pain to tired muscles and fresh blood to the cuts on his shins.

He bound the cuts with strips from the breeks. When he tried to stand again he knew that he did not have the energy to fight another *Alma.*

Not without rest. Not if merely standing is going to take so much effort.

He shuffled on his arse to the nearest wall and leaned back against it, looking down the black maw of the cave.

If an Alma comes now, it could kill me by merely breathing heavily in my direction.

He started to laugh, but did not even have the energy for that. He lay the staff and hammer crossed on his lap and tried to relax. He meant to keep his eyes open, but within seconds a great tiredness washed over him. His head fell forward on his chest.

Seconds later he was sound asleep.

Skald came awake with a start. He'd had no thought of sleeping, but the longer the night had gone on, the more tired he had become, and the old *Alma* had not shown any signs of going to sleep itself. Boredom more than anything had caused Skald to doze.

Dim light came into the cavern from high above. Looking upwards, Skald saw a distant patch of blue sky, thin white cloud dancing across it.

I have slept the night away. It is morning.

He pushed up to his feet, wincing at fresh pain in his leg, having to flex at the knee for several minutes before it would take his weight. The old *Alma* sat and watched him. It looked amused.

"Good morning to you," Skald said sarcastically, and bowed at the waist. The *Alma* hooted with laughter and slapped his palms noisily on the stone beneath it.

Skald sensed movement from the corner of his eye. Beasts were waking and stretching from sleep on the rooftops around him.

The old *Alma* stretched its arms, pushed against the ground and stood, shaky at first, then more assured as it came towards him. It reached out and grabbed Skald's arm, hard enough to bring pain, dragging him across the nest. At the ledge it cradled him in a huge hand, and scrambled down the side of what Skald now saw was another of the tall stone buildings. They swung down using a series of windowsills, headed for the street far below. Across the street three large male *Alma* herded a sorry-looking group of Viking out of a building. They started to push them, none too gently, towards the towering black pillars at the other end of the cavern.

Skald's heart sank. *So it begins.*

Tor woke with a snell wind blowing cold air into his face from the cliff outside. He stood, groaning at aches and pains throughout his whole body. Stiff-legged, he walked to the ruin of his bag. He found some water left in the skin, and some dried fish that could be safely dusted off and eaten. He broke his fast looking out from the cave.

The sun was coming up far to his left, throwing long shadows across the glacier. Far away to his right the fjord glinted in the early sunlight, but both the hut circle and any boats that might be lying offshore, were hidden by the hills between here and there.

I could go back now. Bjorn will have a boat ready.

I could go back, and mayhap be Captain.

From deep in the cave behind him came a rhythmic pounding, like distant drums.

Without any hesitation he took Skald's staff in his left hand, the hammer in his right, and followed the drumbeat down into the darkness.

The old *Alma* led Skald into the space between the buildings that might once have been a street of kinds. A beat rang out around the cavern, stone crashing on stone. As they got closer to the end of the cavern the source of the rhythm soon became apparent. An *Alma* stood in front of each of the black pillars, holding a large rock and hitting it against the stone pillar. The noise reverberated all the way to the ceiling of the cavern. It came back again in a booming echo that rang around them like a great bell.

The old *Alma* stopped when they reached a staircase between the black pillars. The group of *Alma* and their Viking prisoners also came to a halt and stood behind Skald.

The *Alma* at the pillars kept beating on the stone columns as the old one led Skald up the staircase. If Skald could have managed to run he would have fled then and there, fled screaming from the sight he knew was waiting. His stomach tied itself in knots and his bad leg throbbed in time with the beating of stone on stone.

I cannot.

He tried to pull back, but the *Alma* held tightly to his arm and almost dragged him up the rest of the stairs, stopping at the top of the flight.

The drumming of stone against stone stopped and silence fell.

Skald was looking at his nightmare made real. The bastard son of Loki was there only ten yards away. The stone effigy of the huge *Alma* lay on top of the same high plinth he had been shown in the wyrd.

Varni.

Something moved in the wyrd, the red rage of the

berserker he was coming to know intimately. He forced it down.

If I let it come, I will be little more than one of these beasts.

And I am better than that.

I am Viking.

The old *Alma* had also felt the movement in the wyrd. It hooted with laughter then turned to look down the staircase.

It gave out two harsh *chuffs.*

An *Alma* walked forward, passed Skald and headed for the plinth. With one bite it opened up its own arm and let blood drip down onto the stone. The thick red fluid ran down the runnels and hit the stone of the statue. Where it met the effigy, the blood itself turned dark. It *melted*, joining with the rock and hardening.

That is why they need us. Their blood does not work, for they are made of the same stuff as the Jotun. They were made from it.

He did not get time to consider the ramifications. The aged *Alma* chuffed in disappointment, and the bloodied beast returned to join the others, sucking at its wound.

The old one *chuffed* again, twice. In reply two of the beasts grabbed the nearest Viking and dragged him towards the steps.

Some of the men had enough spirit to try to stop them. The *Alma* who were guarding them merely cuffed them aside as if they were no more than excited children that needed to be quietened.

The chosen man wept as he was brought up the steps. He looked straight at Skald, but there was no recognition there. He was one of *Kai*'s lapdogs and had been the bane of Skald's life only months previously, but he looked at Skald as if he had never seen him before.

"Die well. Be a Viking," Skald said as he passed, but there was no reply, only the sound of the man's weeping. The *Alma* dragged the man forward. At the last second the man seemed to wake from his dream and tried to pull away from the beasts. One of the cuffed the man lightly on the head and slung his body onto the plinth.

Only then did he scream, but it was too late for anyone to save him. The *Alma* tore open the still living body with their hands, coolly methodically, disembowelling, tearing. The man's guts were strewn over a wide area of stone, and still he screamed, high wailing screams that Skald knew he would hear for the rest of his life. Blood splattered on and around the plinth...but most ran down the runnels towards the statue.

Where the blood hit it, the stone began to change, lightening in colour, softening. It took on the texture of white hair and pink flesh, soaking up the blood, drinking it in.

The old *Alma* by Skald's side *hooted* in excitement.

The screams suddenly stopped. The two *Alma* kept tearing at the Viking until the flow of blood slowed. Red gore covered the fur of the *Alma*'s thick arms all the way up to their elbows. Blood dripped in a splatter on the stone floor as they walked back past Skald, heading for the group of Viking. This time two men were chosen, the *Alma* lifting them as if they were babes. These men hadn't seen the fate that waited for them -- their view was blocked by the stairs -- but they had heard the tormented screams. They kicked and screamed, trying to tear themselves free, but the *Alma* paid them little mind. Once more the beasts climbed the staircase heading for the plinth.

The Viking met the same fate as the first. Their ribcages were splayed open so that their lights could be fed to the wakening *Jotun*. Their screams echoed high above.

The statue now had a large patch of fur showing, almost the whole length of one of the arms, and beneath it the flesh moved, straining at the rock. Stone cracked and fell away as one of the huge fingers *twitched*.

I cannot allow this to go any further.

Skald pulled hard at the arm of the old male who held him. It looked at him, as if surprised by the rebellion, and cuffed him on the jaw with the other hand, a blow that sent Skald's head spinning.

The red rage washed up in him again, and this time he let it come. He leapt forward, thumbs heading for the beast's eyes.

When he heard the first screams Tor though he might already be too late. They echoed down the tunnel like spectral wails foretelling doom.

I am spending too much time with the Skald.

He started to walk faster, almost a run. The exertions of the day before still clung to his muscles, but as he moved deeper into the cave he started to loosen, and soon he was able to run, full pelt, down into the blackness.

He arrived in a large cavern filled with high vaulted buildings, but he did not have time to stop and appreciate the architecture. The high screaming cut off, but he had already pinpointed its source as being between the tow black pillars that dominated the far end of the cave. He headed for them at a run, expecting at any moment for an *Alma* to step out of the darkness in front of him.

But no one, or no beast, challenged him, and when he arrived at the clear space before the pillars he saw why. All attention was on a tall plinth behind the pillars. Two *Alma* carried Viking warriors up the steps to where an ancient *Alma* stood, holding tight to a slighter figure.

Skald!

As more screams started, twofold and louder, Tor was already running. As he passed the group of Viking he called out.

"Viking, to me. Form a circle."

One of the *Alma* guarding the Viking made a grab at Tor. He felled it with a single blow of the hammer, hitting it right between the eyes. It fell, dead before it hit the ground.

Some of the Viking were fleet of mind enough to

follow Tor as he leapt up the steps. Skald was there, standing over the body of a dead *Alma*. His hands dripped gore and the *Alma* had bloody holes where its eyes had been seconds before. Its head hung limply on its shoulders, showing where Skald had broken its neck.

Skald looked up, and Tor recognised the blank stare.

He is coming out of the wyrd.

"Tor?" Skald said, but Tor had no time to reply.

"Viking. To me," Tor called out again.

There were four men left at the bottom of the steps, all standing as if in a dream.

"To me," Tor called, but it was too late. Three *Alma* pounced, and seconds later the air was filled once more with screams. The noise was terrible, but it did not last long.

Tor looked around.

Two *Alma* were between them and the plinth beyond. Out on the other side stood at least ten more. They seemed confused, staring at the dead *Alma* at Skald's feet.

Skald killed their leader. We may yet get free of this.

But they did not stay leaderless for long. A large male roared, and the rest of them joined in.

"Prepare yourselves," Tor shouted.

The area between the two pillars was too wide to be defended by one man.

But two might hold it. Or at least die valiantly trying.

"Tor?" Skald said again, and this time his eyes were clear. "Is it really you?"

Tor smiled.

"Well met friend." Tor handed Skald his staff.

"Thank you for lending me this," he said. "Now, stand with me, this last time. Valhalla is calling, and I am reluctant to go alone."

Kai was one of the Viking standing beside them. He looked pale and frightened. He pulled the wolf skin cloak around him as if it might somehow offer some protection.

"Skald. Give me the staff. I have no weapon."

Tor laughed.

"You took a perfectly good sword from me. Why do you not use that?"

Then there was no more time for talk.

The *Alma* in front of Tor roared once more, and leapt into the attack.

The Viking held their ground as three *Alma* barrelled into them. Tor managed to step to one side and smack the hammer down on the nearest ones shoulder. The arm immediately went limp and the creature howled in pain. Tor brought down the weapon again and smashed the back of its skull.

Two Viking hung on to another, one at the waist tearing at its groin, the other had got his legs round the beast from the back. He pushed its head down towards its chest in a wrestling hold that Tor recognised from the training ground. The noise of its neck breaking was loud even above the uproar.

Another beast leapt forward, its hand smacking Tor on the head, sending him falling sideways. Talon like nails scratched across the iron studs of his helmet. The other hand of the beast swiped across his vision, missing Tor's face by less than an inch. He felt the wind of its passing, and smelled the stench of damp fur. He lashed out with the hammer at the only target he could reach – the hairy foot of the Alma. The stone head crushed bone, flattening two toes into a mushy pulp.

The beast fell away sideways. One of the Viking grabbed it by the head. He shoved the head into his armpit and *twisted.*

The *Alma* fell, dead.

The Viking threw his head back and roared his victory, but the roar was cut short as a second beast bent over him and bit halfway through his neck, the victory shout turning immediately to a gurgle as blood bubbled form his torn throat. Tor slammed the hammer into the beast's side, breaking ribs. The beast rolled away but it was too late for the Viking. He stared up blindly as Tor spun away to the next attack.

40

The two *Alma* between Skald and the plinth seemed reluctant to advance. Behind him Skald knew that Tor was in a life or death battle, but he could not take his eyes from the beasts. They watched him intently, standing on the balls of their feet. They swayed slightly from side to side. Skald hefted his staff, holding it with hands a foot apart, ready to strike with either end if an attack came.

But still the beasts did not advance. One of them shifted its gaze, looking at the body of the old male at Skald's feet, then looking back to Skald. When it saw that Skald was looking at it, it averted its eyes.

They fear me.

Am I now the pack leader? Is that what this is?

Skald stepped forward.

The beasts took a step back.

He raised the staff, threatening them.

They dropped their heads, subservient.

Skald roared loudly and ran forward two steps, brandishing the staff.

The beasts bounded off into the darkness.

Skald was about to turn, to tell Tor of the development, when a large piece of stone fell from the plinth.

He looked up.

The *Jotun* had come almost halfway out of the stone. His whole left arm, part of his chest and almost all his head showed white, bristling fur. The eyes stared straight at Skald. The great mouth opened, wide enough to swallow Skald whole. He tried to scream, but the rock held his chest too tight, and no noise escaped. More stone crumbled and fell from the body, bringing him closer to escape every second.

"Tor," Skald called. "To me."

41

Tor heard Skald's call, but could not spare the time to turn. A large male *Alma* stood in front of him, crouched in a fighting stance. Tor believed it was the very male who had directed the attacks on the stockade. And this was the beast that now had assumed the leadership of the attack here.

He was aware that only two other Viking still stood beside him. One of them was Kai, who had yet to take any part in the fight, seemingly struck immobile in terror. The other was a small wiry Viking, some four inches shorter than Tor himself, a man from the *Firewyrm.* He fought with a frenzy that equalled that of the beasts, biting as much as bitten. He was covered in wounds, streaming blood, but he roared back at an *Alma* and threw himself at it. It caught him in mid air and pulled him forward. Even as the creature tore his face off he head butted it, hard, bringing it to its knees. The beast broke his back but with his last act he bent forward and bit deep into its neck, tearing the jugular and sending a fountain of blood in the air. The *Alma* staggered, the Viking still clamped to its neck, and finally they fell together, and lay still.

Tor kept his gaze on the big male. It came forward slowly, not taking its eyes from the hammer. It smiled, showing Tor its teeth. Tor smiled back.

He showed it the hammer.

It leapt forward.

Tor tried to jump aside, but his foot caught on a dead beast at his feet. He tripped, going on one knee. The *Alma* screamed in triumph and Tor saw his death coming for him. He started to raise the hammer, but knew it was too late, the beast closed on him too fast.

It showed him his teeth again, opening its mouth

for the killing bite. But it did not come. An arm came into Tor's view and was thrust between him and the gaping maw. When the beast bit down it met the wrist.

Tor looked up.

Kai stood above him, grimacing in pain. Even as the beast chewed on his hand the Viking reached forward with the other and thrust his thumb deep in the *Alma's* eye bringing blood.

The beast howled. It cuffed Kai on the side of the head, caving in his skull.

Kai stared straight at Tor as he fell, his eyes going dim.

"I die Viking," he whispered. It was almost a question.

"Yes," Tor said. "You die Viking."

But the man was already gone, and did not hear him.

Kai's sacrifice had bought Tor enough time to regain his balance. The beast spat Kai's hand to the ground, as if it was unpalatable. Blood ran from the corner of one eye but its roar was as fierce as ever as it aimed a blow at Tor's head.

He ducked under it and hammered the stone weapon into its belly. It was a sound stroke, and raised a *chuff* of pain from the *Alma*. He had not hit any bones, but blood came at the beast's lips. It held a hand across its stomach and moaned. It pushed itself upright and *screamed* in pain. Blood poured from its mouth and ran down its chest.

Tor smiled grimly as it came at him again.

He ducked under another swinging arm and pounded it in the stomach again, but this time it was waiting for him. It grabbed the hammer and wrenched it from his hand. Tor tried to roll away but a huge foot kicked him, hard. A rib cracked. Tor tasted blood in his own mouth as he smacked into one of the black pillars.

The beast loomed over him.

Tor waited for the killing blow.

It never came.

The beast stood still as a roar echoed around the cavern.

42

Skald saw the *Alma's* kick and watched in horror as Tor slammed hard into the pillar. He held his breath until he saw Tor struggle to his knees. The beast raised its foot for another kick, one that would stomp Tor into the ground and crush his chest to a pulp.

Skald raised the staff above his head and roared.

All movement in the cavern stopped. The only sound was the tumble of stone from the plinth behind him, but Skald did not have time to look around.

He stared straight at the big male that stood over Tor, never taking his eyes off it.

It stared back.

It raised itself to its full height and thumped its palms on its chest.

Skald stood quiet, but he never let his eyes stray from those of the beast.

Tor staggered to his feet and made for the hammer.

"No," Skald shouted. "This one is mine."

If Tor had laughed then it might have gone differently, but he nodded to Skald and leaned back against the pillar, coughing, then spitting some bloody phlegm at the *Alma*'s feet.

Skald showed the beast the staff again, and let out a roar that echoed through the cavern and brought more flecks of snow from high above.

He took two running steps forward.

But the trick that had worked with the other two did not work with this one. It drew back its lips and laughed at him. It dropped into a wrestler's crouch and walked forward, once more tensing and relaxing its hands.

Skald stood his ground, wielding the wood in his hands like a quarterstaff. He knew he did not have the dexterity to escape if it came to close fighting – his bad leg would hamper him too much for that. So he stood, eye to eye as the *Alma* came on.

He roared as it got to within six feet of him, surprising the beast such that it stopped, curious. Skald led the wood slip quickly through his palms then swung, with all the force he could muster. The beast tried to duck away but the staff caught it flush on the side of the head and more blood flew from its mouth.

Skald brought the wood back.

He thrust the staff, like a sword, deep into the *Alma's* belly. Already wounded there by the blow Tor had given it, it collapsed to its knees, spewing up gouts of blood at Skald's feet.

It turned its head and stared at him. It opened its mouth, tried to roar, but only a mewling wail came out and even that stopped as blood filled its mouth.

"Skald," he heard Tor cry.

He looked up, and Tor threw him the hammer.

He caught it on the rise and brought it down in the same action, right between the beast's eyes, the stone following through into the skull in a spray of brain and bone.

Skald raised his head and roared.

Tor turned, expecting an attack from the remaining *Alma*, but they all stood silent. They looked towards Skald who stood arms raised, the bloody hammer in one hand and the staff in the other.

Then Tor realised it was *not Skald* they watched.

It was the giant figure that tried to rise up from the rock behind him. It looked like a huge *Alma*, one that would tower thirty feet high or more if it ever got upright, and it had started to push itself out of the rock it was encased in.

And that is something we cannot allow.

He staggered over to *Skald*'s side.

"What in Odin's name must we fight now? What is this thing?"

At first Tor thought Skald would not answer, but finally his friend whispered.

"He is like me."

Skald did not elaborate. He left Tor's side and walked towards the giant.

"What do we do?" Tor said. "Can we kill it?"

Skald looked back at him, then over his shoulder. His eyes widened.

"I am not sure *we* will have to do anything."

Tor looked round, expecting an attack.

A large group of the small fur clad people walked up the staircase towards him, the old woman Baren in the lead.

Baren walked up to Skald, stretched and rapped him on the forehead.

He heard the words from the wyrding in his head.

You have come from the north to lead us back to the place of the digging, where we will once more be one with the Father.

Some of the small people had already walked past them. They clambered up on the plinth and pressed their bodies against the places where the stone had turned to fur. Where they touched, they *melted*, flesh turning grey, hardening, their bones and blood, even their furs being incorporated into the rock.

The *Jotun* thrashed and screamed, dislodging rock and bringing more snowflakes down on them from high above. Slowly, inexorably, the stone crept through the fur, hardening and blackening. More of the people climbed on the plinth, clambering over the already hard bodies of their brethren to reach the exposed fur. They too melted and hardened, giving all of themselves to the stone. They smiled as it took them.

Soon all had gone to the rock except Baren.

She took Skald's hand. She had tears in her eyes, tears of joy. She hugged him tight. She smiled up at him, then waddled to the plinth and clambered, high up, until she was level with the face of the *Jotun*. One huge eye glared at her. She patted a hand on the giant's cheek, and fell against it. Flesh turned to stone.

She looked back one last time, then she was gone.

Blackness crept until all trace of white was erased and there was only the gnarled rock, the bodies of the people indistinguishable from each other where they entwined with the *Jotun*.

Skald and Tor stood, waiting to see if anything else

might happen, but there was only stone and the soft snow falling from above.

"What just happened?" Tor asked quietly.

Skald watched the rock for a long time but there was no movement.

"They have gone to sleep with their father," Skald said, and turned away so that Tor would not see his tears.

45

They had plenty of time to talk on their slow trek back to the settlement, but they passed most of it in silence, each lost in their own thoughts, their own pain.

No *Alma* followed. Indeed, they had seen none since back in the cavern. After the *Jotun* was taken by the rock the beasts had lost all interest in the Viking. When Tor and Skald walked back through the streets pale eyes watched them, but did not approach. Instead they shrank back into the shadows, heads lowered in subservience.

The climb down the cliff proved taxing, but Tor led the way, helping Skald find handholds, taking it slowly.

They walked across the glacier by night while the sky sang and hissed with colour and the Gods walked above.

At one point Tor asked Skald what had happened. The reply did not make much sense to Tor. Skald told of *Loki,* and a child who tried to be free of its bonds.

"The small people were made first," Skald said. "But there was too much of his father and not enough of his mother in them. So he tried again, with the *Alma.*"

Skald had looked at Tor, tears once more in his eyes.

"I am like them," he said softly. "I am like them all."

He would say no more.

Skald's mood only improved when, on the afternoon of the second day, tired and pained, they walked out of the forest onto the shore by the stockade.

A boat lay on the water, sail flapping in the wind. Sail-master Bjorn hailed them from the bow.

"Well met Viking."

Tor raised the hammer and Skald raised his staff, and the four Viking aboard the boat banged against the deck in welcome. They waded out to the boat, almost running. Bjorn leaned over and helped them aboard.

Five minutes later they sat at a brazier, drinking hot stew and telling their tale. By the time they had finished the stew was doing its job and both Tor and Skald were in danger of falling asleep.

Bjorn handed Tor a long sword.

"This belonged to the Captain of the *Firewyrm*. It is now yours, by right of your courage."

Tor shook his head.

"There is another Viking more deserving."

He hefted the hammer he had used in the battle with the *Alma*.

"This will do for me," he said.

He took the sword and offered it to Skald.

Skald nodded, took it, and gave it a few practice swings.

"We are Viking," Skald said quietly.

Tor smiled.

"We are Viking. But even Viking must sleep."

"Before that, we must decide on a course of action," the sail-master said.

"Home," Tor replied. "Home to Ormsdale. Our Skald has tales of glory to tell in the Great Hall."

Tor's head nodded forward onto his chest and blissful sleep beckoned, but he raised a smile as he heard Bjorn's next words.

"Whatever you ask, *Captain*."

End

About the Author

William Meikle is a Scottish writer, now living in Canada, with twenty novels published in the genre press and over 300 short story credits in thirteen countries. His works span a variety of genres, including Horror, Fantasy, Mystery, and Science Fiction.

Try these thrilling titles from Gryphonwood!

The Absent Gods Trilogy by David Debord

Centuries ago, the land of Gameryah was saved from the forces of the Ice King by the Silver Serpent. Now the frost marches again and three young villagers set off on a perilous quest to recover the legendary weapon. Join Shanis Malan, a rebellious young woman, Oskar Klehn a bookish misfit, and Hierm Van Derin, an outcast second son, in a classic fantasy in the tradition of David Eddings and Robert Jordan, filled with magic, intrigue, and adventure!

Written in Blood by Ryan A. Span

The darkest secrets can afford to wait...

Karl Byren has fallen a long way since his youth in the King's Army. Washed up, reduced to mercenary work and alcoholism, he scrapes out a living as a 'Contractor,' a kind of hired bodyguard for whom the job is more important than his life. It's a dangerous trip through the heart of a civil war and into places beyond Byren's wildest imaginations. Everyone knows there's no such thing as magic — but it's starting to get too close for comfort.

A dark epic fantasy in the tradition of Mark Lawrence and Game of Thrones!

Flank Hawk by Terry W. Ervin II

What happens when fire-breathing dragons battle Stukas for aerial supremacy over a battlefield? Can an earth wizard's magic defeat a panzer? Krish, a farmhand turned mercenary, witnesses this and much more as he confronts the Necromancer King's new war machines resurrected from before the First Civilization's fall. Worse yet, a wounded prince tasks Krish to find the fabled Colonel of the West and barter the royal family's malevolent Blood-Sword for a weapon to thwart the Necromancer King's victory. Flank Hawk is set in the distant future where magic exists and brutish ogres are more than a child's nightmare.

Epic fantasy in the tradition of Terry Brooks!

The Valley by William Meikle

A lost world has been found again... and no one is getting out alive.

1863, a group of mercenaries in Montana come upon the remains of a once-thriving mining town. They soon discover that the destruction was not wrought by human hands, but by creatures long forgotten. William Meikle delivers a classic Lost World story with just the right touch of Horror and Western. You'll be on the edge of your seat as you descend into The Valley.

Made in the USA
Las Vegas, NV
26 September 2021